# Fading of
# the
# Symphonies

## Chapter One

A heavy and persistent rain beat relentlessly against the window pane as a svelte figure leaned over his desk to switch off the light, around five feet ten in height and slim in build Charlie was running late, placing his black dinner jacket over his pearl coloured shirt and black bow tie he used the reverse angle of the camera on his smart phone as a mirror whilst he brushed his hair. The strong hair products he had used that morning was beginning to relent its ability to hold the style he wanted.

The black multi functioning phone sounded its dull repetitive ring until he picked up the receiver. "Charlie Marshall" he responded to the caller on the other end of the line. "I know I'm late, I'm on my way" Charlie insisted quickly checking his watch realising just how late he was. "Ok…Ok five minutes" he concluded dropping the receiver and reaching for his coat on a nearby hook.

As Charlie did so he felt a sharp and searing pain strike across his abdomen like a warm knife piercing through his skin, clutching his side he eased himself back upright from the doubled over position he found himself in knowing the pain would eventually pass. And he was right, it did because Charlie already knew its cause, almost five months before he had developed a hernia but with his hectic and antisocial work life he hadn't got around to going to the doctors.

Reaching the foyer he hurried toward the exit almost slipping on the recently polished reflective marble floor beneath his feet and as he did so, signalled goodnight to the rather rotund night watchmen who locked the door behind him, leaving Charlie out in the hostile elements of a cold London night. Pulling the collar up on his winter coat to prevent the lashing rainwater hitting his neck he prayed for a taxi, a dozen or so passed each with their top lights turned off signalling they already had a fare, seemingly everyone had the same idea as him.

It was just Charlie's luck that the one night of the year he couldn't afford to be late, he was stuck in the rain and with only one option he'd have to make a run for it.

Charlie was a young up and comer at a large and commercially successful publishing company based in central London, he had worked his way up the company ladder from lowly intern to a senior agent in little under a decade, he had been noted as being determined to climb the corporate ladder with a rather tenacious and dogged desire to succeed and finally all of his hard work had paid off, he'd been recognised.

With a position to become senior partner up for grabs the partners had given Charlie the chance to prove himself by attracting a new and commercially successful client to the company, a task also given to another hopeful Jason Kraft, who was as determined as Charlie to progress and had seen him as his main competition ever since he'd arrived at the company. Jason saw the business and profession as much more cut throat than Charlie and would sink to any dirty and underhanded tactic to get an advantage but this time his approach had backfired and the contract for a global best selling author and poet had gone to Charlie to represent her, feeling his honesty and professionalism as well as his personality would suit her better than Jason's aggressive and go for the throat mentality.

And now a party to celebrate Charlie and the companies success in landing such a huge client was underway at the Marriot Hotel and Charlie was missing it, running through the busy and traffic ridden streets avoiding the swift forming puddles the best he could with the umbrella wielding masses either shopping or trying to get home after a long day at work.

Turning the corner on to County Hall Road the garish lights of the Marriot's entrance shone in the dark like a beacon guiding him to his destination. As Charlie got closer he noticed a familiar face, huddled beneath a umbrella and a white filtered cigarette clenched between her thick red painted lips.

"Where the bloody hell have you been?" she asked sounding rather agitated as he approached, taking a final drag she cast the cigarette to the ground extinguishing it beneath her heel.

"I know, I know, I was waiting on a call over the new contract" Charlie bemoaned a little relieved that he'd made it.

"Well you're here now…I suppose" the women in her mid forties grumbled, closing the umbrella in the doorway she immediately began patting the back and sides of her long self curled hair that had been pinned up in to an elegant looking bun, making sure not even a single strand was out of place before fiddling with the narrow straps of her sleeveless scarlet red gown, fitted to perfection around her slim yet curvaceous figure whilst extenuating her ample cleavage.

Charlie was taken by the arm and led inside the Marriot's rather opulent reception and in to the hotels grand ballroom where seemingly no expense had been spared, professionally decorated for the occasion it was a lesson in the lavish side of society. It had been seen as a massive coup from Charlie to have lured such a huge and commercially successful and internationally well known author as Belinda Thomas, the so called "Queen of the thriller" and crime writer extraordinaire from her previous representatives and the companies' partners wanted the party to highlight that success.

Sixty or so guests from employees and their spouses to the companies shareholders were in attendance and sat around the dozen large circular tables, the more important and distinguished guests had been allocated seats closer to the stage area that had been erected especially for the occasion with a narrow perspex stand in the middle and a black microphone holstered in its top. The three Michelin star cuisine was consumed heartily, enjoyed more by the staff than the partners and so called dignitaries, seeing it as such a luxury to experience such extravagant cuisine by a recognised chef whom had been prominent on television, with appearances on countless cookery programs and one ill fated reality show.

For most in attendance at the black tie affair the situation felt alien and uncomfortable each of them feeling somewhat out of their league, none more so than Charlie who had been seated toward the back of the room, the table was almost fully consumed by shadow.

Seated with the seven members of his team, most of them had been at the company almost as long as he had, getting on well as a team both professionally and personally they often made frequent trips to the closest pub to the office after particular stressful days, which in their line of work was more common than they would have liked to admit.

All of them were either in or entering their thirties and mostly unmarried. "Married to the job" as the saying goes and all that it entailed, the long nights, the weekends and the seemingly constant travelling. Laughing and conversing between themselves whilst their dinner plates were removed and their glasses refilled by the more than obliging serving staff as Sir Hector Doors, grandson of Clarence Doors founder of the company ascended the make shift stage along with two of the female partners, each donning their finest attire.

The thin withered faces of Henrietta Bowbridge and Dame Cynthia Jenkins-Smith scanned the audience with an icy stare, they deemed themselves far too superior to converse with the minions of the company, the so called minions whose hard work had helped to provide them with their opulent and rather fantastic lifestyles.

The task of addressing the seated employees had befallen to Sir Hector, a tall underweight man in his mid sixties with sharp pointed features and reseeding white hair, a little eccentric in behaviour and deeply proud of his family name and the distinguished heritage that came with it.

"Ladies, gentlemen and guests, welcome" his wispy voice complete with upper class twang sprang in to life, its mere sound brought the large rooms inhabitants to a courteous and respectful silence as he held his hands a loft in a stopping gesture, his broad smile revealed his pristinely polished dentures.

"Tonight we celebrate a momentous occasion for our humble little publishing house" Sir Hector began reading from his pre-typed cards through a pair of small gold rimmed spectacles that balanced precariously on the end of his narrow nose. "With the signing of Belinda Thomas, one of the most critically acclaimed and commercially successful authors of this generation we have cemented ourselves as not only the biggest publishing house in Great Britain but in the western hemisphere" Hector paused for the expected and somewhat forced round of a applause, taking it in as if he was the intended beneficiary of the adulation before requesting quiet once more.

"For this wonderful achievement we must acknowledge the hard work of Charlie Marshall and his team for without their tireless efforts and contribution what we are celebrating this evening would not have been possible".

As Hector concluded, a bright white spotlight illuminated the overshadowed table in a well rehearsed manoeuvre and in doing so allowed all eyes from the other guests to focus in on Charlie who with a slight push in the small of his back was on his feet, immediately feeling rooted to the spot and not knowing what to do as the applause resonated even louder than before.

Charlie felt he was in hell as he loathed being the centre of attention but for him it was only going to get worse as he noticed Sir Hector signalling to join him on the stage with a gesture of his fingers being repeatedly folded back and fourth in to his hand, tentatively Charlie walked between the tables before nervously taking to the stage, receiving a generic handshake from the three senior partners as he did so, each of them could sense the photo opportunity like a shark sensing droplets of blood in the ocean.

Thinking the meaningless thank you for his deeds and picture opportunity to go on someone's office wall was all that was required of him Charlie was about to make a swift return to his seat but was immediately halted by Sir Hector as his head lowered toward the microphone once more.

"Charlie Marshall began working here at Doors and Handley almost ten years ago, taking an internship with us from university…I believe" began Sir Hector once more, looking to Charlie who hesitantly nodded, indicating to the old man that his secretary who presumably had written his speech had her facts correct.

"We as a family business took him under our wing and gave him the knowledge and the tools that has allowed him to flourish" he beamed with pride at his own waffling nonsense as his bored yet obligated audience pretended to listen intently. "Rising up the corporate ladder under our watchful eye Charlie Marshall has demonstrated the vigour and enthusiasm that this company has been built upon since its inception over seventy years ago, and it is believed by myself and fellow partners that Charlie has the potential to drive Doors and Handley even further, encompassing new territory in the publishing world for years to come…" he paused for needed breath, believing his speech was original and riveting in Sir Hectors mind he was right up there with Churchill and Kennedy, capable of rallying millions with his words if he so intended.

Sipping at his swift fizzing champagne he readied himself to continue. "And with that said I would like to announce that Charlie Marshall is to become our new senior partner, and in doing so becoming the youngest partner Doors and Handley has ever had".

Sir Hector led the applause and as like a bush fire it gathered with momentum until the entire room echoed with the repeated slapping of hands especially from Charlie's team, all of whom had enjoyed more than their fair share of complimentary bottles of champagne and a wide range of alcohol from the free bar.

Overwhelmed and riddled with nervousness Charlie was ushered toward the glass podium by Sir Hector with an indication that a few words would be required, feeling like a rabbit caught in the headlights and with public speaking something Charlie detested the most he tried to formulate some sort of reply in his head, something adequate enough to use to address his peers and bosses alike knowing it had to be both eloquent and intellectual but Charlie's mind was drawing a blank.

With the applause and adulation now suppressed it was now time for Charlie to begin, he squinted his eyes under the bright spotlight its warmth causing him to perspire a little as he noticed Jason sitting in his line of sight, his arms folded tightly across his chest and an expression of disinterest and distain etched on his face.

His hands grasped either side of the podium and leaned a little forwards, a decision he instantly regretted as a shock of sheer pain jetted from the side of his stomach just as it had done back at the office, feeling immediately uneasy but knowing the people were waiting for him to speak Charlie knew he had to pull it together.

"Where to start?" he quietly began, the odd sound of his own voice amplified in his ears from the microphone. "It is a great honour to be made a senior partner" Charlie continued suddenly feeling irregular his skin tingled as if every hair on his body was standing on end beneath his clothing, perspiring a cold sweat he glanced down at the odd sensation that seemed to occupy his right arm. Charlie's hand was trembling almost uncontrollably and no matter how hard he tried he couldn't stop his freely twitching limbs, his eyes widened with an instinctive and natural fear. "Err…Err" Charlie stammered trying not to draw attention to what was happening to him.

"I would like to thank my team" Charlie stopped himself again knowing something was seriously wrong, staring out in to the lilac and pearl decorated room his distress laid bare for all to see as the colour drained from his face.

The tremor in his right hand spread to the left as Charlie tried to loosen his tie, feeling stifled and claustrophobic but as he did so a droplet of blood impacted on his hand from his nose then another spec then another, stricken with panic he looked to his friends and peers who seemed to mirror

Charlie's own horrified expression, even Jason had become perturbed and concerned, poised on the edge of his seat as if ready to leap in to action and it was a good job he was too as Charlie swayed back and fourth his eyes clamped shut.

Suddenly he blacked out and fell forwards knocking over the fake glass podium with a crash, as he did so Jason instinctively dropped to his knees enabling himself to catch Charlie's top half, preventing him from hitting his head on the soon to be dance floor as a crowd hurriedly surrounded them. Amongst the gasps of concern and frantic search for anyone capable of first aid the women who had awaited Charlie outside the Marriot kneeled beside his unconscious body, her phone was flush to her ear as she called the emergency services.

## Chapter Two

Charlie's eyes slowly opened whilst every part of his body ached, he felt terrible as if he'd been on the receiving end of a welter weights boxing glove, picking up the scent of disinfectant in his nostrils and a high pitched bleeping sounding in his ears instinctively Charlie knew he was in hospital, examining his arms, hands and chest to see tubes and wires penetrating and protruding through them, the image of Frankenstein's monster entered his head.

His vision was blurred and a little distorted as if something was restricting his sight but Charlie immediately recognised the problem was his contact lenses had been removed, slowly looking around the near vicinity of his bed Charlie vaguely made out the outline of his black framed glasses, taking more effort than it was usually required for him to trigger movement in his arms, he made a lurching movement for the glasses succeeding in his second attempt.

Once back in position in the middle of the grey steel framed bed he placed them over his eyes, everything began to ease back in to focus allowing him to see the glum hospital where he found himself in its entirety. The ward was grey and dull and matched the weather outside perfectly it was sparsely inhabited with only three other beds occupied, two were unconscious and hooked up to machines monitoring them as they slept whilst the third who was an elderly gentlemen in a blue chequered dressing gown was sat in a tall backed red chair in the corner of the long narrow room beside the window, watching television with a pair of beige hospital acquired earphones fixed over his ears.

Charlie's legs seemed to be suffering temporary paralysis due to their lack of use but with effort eventually they began to obey his commands allowing him enough movement to help him sit upright, the coarse sheets rubbed and agitated his skin as he did so. The odd and rather uncomfortable sensation of cheap sheets, flat pillows and cold uncomfortable beds triggered pained and repressed memories for Charlie, memories of a childhood spent mostly in hospital and of tests and treatments over a five year period as he battled against Leukaemia, a battle he had finally won at the age of eleven.

Striving to find something close to the feeling of comfort Charlie accidently pulled out one of the wires attached to his chest triggering the once dormant machine beside his bed to bleep an extremely loud, constant and monotonous sound. Almost a minute had passed before a nurse hurriedly appeared, large and robust and in her late fifties with a rather flustered expression as if she was in the middle of ten different jobs at once.

Without saying a word she reattached the wire and reset the program and alarm before administering a quick yet thoroughly toughened once over, checking his pulse and vital signs before pulling limbs back and fourth, Charlie likened it more to a mugging than an examination, as quick as she appeared the heavy set medical provider hurriedly departed the ward to answer another bleeping machine, to another helpless soul needing her expertise.

Left alone yet again Charlie felt stuck and frustrated and trust to the bed by the wires and tubes that monitored every motion his body had to offer both internally and externally, no-one of senior authority was around no-one to answer the questions that ate away at him. "What had caused him to collapse, and how long had he been languishing in that bed?"

Looking to his bedside yet again somewhat deflated and dejected he saw a dozen or so get well soon cards, mostly from work and a large bunched arrangement of flowers evenly divided between two narrow necked jars, they had been there a while, so long so that they had begun to wilt, Charlie knew they had to be a generic gift from work, he'd seen the same sort of arrangement given to a work colleague who had suffered a heart attack at his desk and for another who had just given birth, his suspicions confirmed once seeing the small gold leafed card with the Doors and Handley looped initials on its front.

Flipping the card face down Charlie rubbed the back of his aching neck and face whilst the sound of a weeks worth of stubble upon his cheeks and chin emanated in his ears, Charlie began to feel restless and a little redundant as finally a doctor appeared. An Asian women in her mid forties headed for his bed her gold plated pen rested between her teeth as she revised Charlie's chart and case notes, her open white coat revealing the expensive charcoal coloured suite beneath it.

"Good morning Mr Marshall, how are we feeling?" the doctor asked in her broad northern accent, reminiscent of North Yorkshire. "You had us worried" she continued closing the metal folder with a snap.

"I've been better" Charlie remarked but she wasn't listening as without warning she pulled back his bed sheets allowing the cold air to strike his once warm skin causing him to shudder slightly. Becoming used to the new temperature he was being subjected to, his light blue robe was opened revealing to Charlie an elongated scar running down the side of his stomach, the risen lump that had been the size of a mango that he'd self diagnosed on the internet as a hernia had been removed leaving in its place a four and a half inch incision that was pink and angry, looking down a little wide eyed the first thought Charlie had was that the scar resembled a zip.

"How long have I been here?" he asked watching the doctor closely examining and admiring her own work, he held in his stomach a little immediately regretting not going to the gym more often.

Feeling relatively pleased with how it was healing she returned the sheets back to their previous position. "Day number eleven" she finally responded once rechecking Charlie's chart. "We placed you in an induced coma Mr Marshall to help with your recovery, it also allowed us to run the tests we needed to find out what was going on internally" the doctor replied placing her pen in the pocket of her white coat, resting it neatly beside her laminated I.D badge that contained a rather unflattering picture and her name. "Anita Patel".

"And?" Charlie asked tentatively as Dr Patel rested herself on the side of the bed.

"The growth we removed from your side, we tested it and found it to be" she began before being suddenly interrupted.

"Its cancer…isn't it" Charlie quietly answered with a sigh, receiving a slow nod of the head from the doctor, somewhere in the recesses of his mind Charlie had always thought the lump in his stomach could have been the big C experiencing some of the similar symptoms he had as a child. But the traumatic experience of the invasive medication and chemotherapy coupled with the pain and suffering that the disease had brought him so early in his life made the mere thought of it returning terrifying enough for Charlie to shy away from acknowledging the severity of it, burying his head in the sand and hoping it was nothing more than a simple hernia.

"I've been reading your previous notes and I learned you suffered with Leukaemia almost twenty years ago" said Dr Patel, receiving a nod of concurrence from her panicked looking patient. "And statistically since previously having a form of the disease you were always in the higher percentages to contract a form of the disease again" she explained, her voice quiet with professional compassion and commiseration.

Lightly clenching his tongue between his teeth Charlie exhaled trying to take in and process what Dr Patel was explaining to him. "Well I fought it the last time…so I guess I can do it again" he finally responded with a vigour of defiance and optimism, it was something Dr Patel wasn't expecting.

"I'm afraid it's not that simple Mr Marshall" she protested. "I was able to remove the cancerous tumour and the surrounding contaminated cells but secondary cells have been located in your brain, primarily in the frontal parietal lobe.

"Right…" Charlie slowly responded as he tried to comprehend the new information, trying to act as strong and collected as he could whilst not wanting to show any weakness or emotion in front of the doctor but his eyes were rife with fear and inconsolable despair.

"Then where do we go from here?" he asked sounding a little lost as Charlie's mind was flush with the suppressed memories of his childhood, all of the pain and struggle he had once thought would never return was now back with a vengeance.

"Well I would like to keep you in for a few more days at least" answered Dr Patel. "It will allow us to run more tests and see just what we are up against and how we can accordingly fight the disease" she elaborated her professional manner and tone of voice did nothing to raise Charlie's spirits and more importantly hope.

Charlie was about to ask another question when he saw two familiar faces in the doorway of the ward, linked arm in arm the couple in their late twenties immediately made a bee line for his bed.

"Err ok…aright" he quickly responded to Dr Patel in a rather hushed tone. "Do whatever you need" he concluded with a nod.

"Hey, hey alright mate" the man called reaching the foot of Charlie's bed, his round and rather chubby face a mixture of joy and excitement seeing Charlie was awake.

Standing well over six feet and almost double the size of Charlie the over friendly man headed around the bed to hug him, his bear like grip and hold enveloped Charlie's still sore and aching body causing him to wince slightly.

"Careful" called the female, she was a rather slight thing only a little over five feet and with a petite frame, smooth olive skin and shoulder length black hair that shined in the overhead lighting of the hospital ward scooped back in to a ponytail. "Remember he's just had surgery" she continued prizing them apart before giving Charlie a peck on the cheek, rubbing away the dark lipstick mark she had with made her thumb.

"So how's he doing doc?" the man asked rather loud and exuberantly as he and the women took to the chairs beside the bed.

Dr Patel remained tight lipped as she stood beside Charlie her gaze tracked on his as her vow of doctor, patient confidentiality prevented her from saying anything without his say so and Charlie knew that fact. In that moment Charlie knew he was at a crossroads with a moral dilemma, he couldn't decide whether to tell them the truth that he had been diagnosed with the terrible disease or to spare them the sadness and somewhat despair that he himself felt.

"I'm going to be alright" Charlie chose the latter to spare his friends. "I'm just exhausted and over stressed…what with work and the hernia…but I'm getting better" he lied, seeing the immediate look of relief on their faces as he did so.

Charlie felt bad for lying to his two closest friends but knew in the long run it would be for the best, knowing they would find out the truth eventually, he chose for them to find out later rather than sooner. He and Tommy had known one another since nursery school and were more like brothers than friends, Tommy had been with him the last time he was seriously ill and had been left as traumatised as Charlie had been, with the intense and aggressive disease and treatment but the experience had only served to create a stronger bond between them. Charlie had met Lydia at university and had been the one to introduce her to Tommy, she was a mother hen figure to the both of them, seeing it as her duty to keep a watchful eye over Charlie as well as keeping him in check.

Being raised by his grandparents after his mothers death when he was two and never knowing his father, Tommy and Lydia were the closest Charlie had to a family, the few serious relationships he'd had never amounted to anything lasting, causing Charlie to put all of his attention in to his job that helped suppressed the thoughts of a life with someone to go home to at night, someone to love, someone to spend his life with.

"You're going to be alright" Tommy repeated, receiving a slight nod of concurrence from Charlie as Dr Patel made her quiet retreat from his bed to give them some privacy. "I'm so relieved" he smiled a rather jovial smile as a surge of relief and excitement rushed through Tommy's rather heavy set frame.

"I've got to stay in a few more days, then I should be ready to go home" Charlie answered trying to deviate his deception by turning his attention to a beaker of iced orange juice and an over turned glass on the cabinet beside his bed, his throat and mouth becoming dry.

"Don't overstretch…I'll do it" ordered Lydia immediately leaping from her chair to pour Charlie a drink, her mothering instinct sprang in to action.

Watching the juice disappear from the glass Lydia replaced it on the cabinet. "You scared us to death" she continued whilst helping Charlie get as close to comfortable as he could. "You were unconscious for so long we were starting to think that you wouldn't wake up, and because we're not technically family nobody would tell us anything" Lydia concluded not fully convinced that Charlie was telling them the whole truth about what was really going on, she'd always been able to tell when Charlie was hiding something and he knew it.

"They want me to stay in for a few more days so they can run some tests" Charlie felt compelled to elaborate whilst feeling Lydia's probing stare fixed upon him.

"Tests…what sort of tests?" yelped Tommy almost choking on the mouthful of grapes he'd liberated from the nearby fruit bowl.

"It's nothing serious" Charlie soothed. "Dr Patel wants to run a few more tests to see what caused me to pass out" he continued flippantly watching Tommy's rigid stance begin to ease back in to his chair. "She's ninety nine percent sure that it was brought on by stress and fatigue…that's all, I'll be fine" Charlie concluded hoping his own false reassurance would stem his friend's curiosity.

And it had seemed to work as Lydia's line of questioning ceased and before too long the subject had changed to one of a more light hearted nature.

Five days passed and countless tests on his body and blood taken as well as a photo album of C.T scans of his brain and yet Charlie seemed no closer to being discharged or further diagnosed. Free of the restricting wires and tubes fixing him to the bed Charlie became more mobile he was able to walk around a little as well as getting himself in and out of bed and using the bathroom unassisted. Sitting cross legged upon the bed he now considered his own given the amount of time he had spent in it, Charlie read the newspaper and too preoccupied on reading the latest news on the middle eastern conflict to notice Dr Patel hovering in the doorway, a few moments more passed before she advanced holding a light blue folder under her arm.

"Good morning Mr Marshall" spoke Patel in her no nonsense regional accent, the sound caused Charlie to look up from the black and white print before him.

"Morning" he replied with a courteous and polite smile.

"How are you feeling today?" she continued with a look a genuine interest.

"I'm good...the new medication seems to be doing the job" Charlie sounded upbeat and optimistic, the pain he'd accustomed himself to was now nothing more than a dull ache.

"Good...that's good" said Dr Patel, the accomplished surgeon and leading consultant at the London Bridge Hospital harboured a steely expression as her hand gripped the blue curtain beside the bed. "I have your test results" she continued walking around the bed with the curtain trailing in her grasp, she thought their conversation warranted privacy.

Cocooned within the nylon curtain Charlie's mood instantly transformed in to one of worry and the doctors wanting of privacy only heightened the sense that the forth coming news couldn't be good.

"I'm sorry but the tests show the worst prognosis we could have hoped for, you have metastatic brain cancer, it is a common tumour but we are unable to operate due to its location and the aggressiveness of the cancerous cells" Dr Patel explained and hating every moment of doing so, it was the worst part of the job for her.

Charlie was shell shocked, rocked to his very core. "You mean...I'm dying?" he stammered his voice started to break as he uttered the sentence as an immediate feeling of nausea seemed to surge from his stomach and in to his throat, leaving Charlie overbearingly flustered.

"I'm afraid so yes" Patel replied with a slow nod of the head. "It is too volatile and removing it is impossible, I fear you wouldn't make it through the surgery" she continued with her explanation. Charlie slowly nodded, his head lowered towards his lap as he tried to contain the panic and fear he was experiencing." How...how long have I got?" he asked managing to force the words out even though the thought of the answer he would receive petrified him.

"It's difficult to say" the doctor's voice lowered to a tone of sympathy. "By the rate of how quick and aggressive the type of cancer you have is, my prognosis is between six and nine months…but with careful observation and the right medication then maybe a year".

With his mind blank and blocked by his terror Charlie was finding it difficult to comprehend and process the information, feeling as if his soul had been ripped clean from his body, the thought of himself dying and with nothing he could do to prevent it left Charlie with a pained and powerless feeling. As if switching to autopilot Charlie's face was bereaved of emotion and his body was rooted to the spot as if petrified in stone and not allowing even the slightest of movement from his limbs, for the first time in his life Charlie felt completely alone and inconsolably lost.

"I'm sorry Mr Marshall, I wish there was something we could do" began Dr Patel a little unnerved but not surprised by Charlie's reaction, in her profession she had seen every reaction from people once hearing terrible news, from the angry and the dispossessed to the calm, positive and proactive, she knew only too well just how different every patient was. "Have you any questions, anything you want to ask or want to know?" she continued poised and ready to answer anything that came her way.

Waiting a few moments and Charlie's response came by a short shake of the head. "Ok" she conceded before heading toward the exit of the curtain.

"No…wait" Charlie finally spoke halting the doctor in her tracks. "What will happen to me…before I die, I mean?" he quietly asked, his eyes fixed forwards towards the bottom of the bed feeling unable to make eye contact.

"Will it hurt…will my body stop working?" Charlie stammered a little whilst panicking at the thought of what could happen to him. "Please tell me I won't be trapped in my own body!" he almost shrieked, his body trembled in an all consuming fear.

Dr Patel thought for a moment or two searching for an easier way to tell him of what he was likely to experience, but the truth was there was no easier way of describing what horror's Charlie could experience from such an aggressive and volatile disease.

"We can never be one hundred per cent sure of what will happen because every person and every case is different but previous records of your condition show symptoms of sporadic blood loss from the brain via the nose, mouth and ears, seizures could be a possibility and tremors of the limbs and in the very worst cases there has been situations where patients have suffered both permanent and temporary blindness as the brain slowly degenerates".

With what possibly lay ahead for him every instinct in Charlie's body told him to run, just run away and hope the problem couldn't follow him, the thought of himself going blind was the last straw he couldn't bare to hear anymore. "I have to get out of here" he called leaping from the bed his body still trembling with the raw terror from the threat of the cancer consuming him. "I can't stay here anymore, I want to go home" Charlie continued defiantly.

"Please Mr Marshall get back in to bed" asked Dr Patel. "I want to keep you in for just a few days more".

But her protests fell upon deaf ears as she watched Charlie retrieve some folded clothes that Tommy and Lydia had brought him from home out of the cupboard beside him.

"Please…it's for your own good" she tried again but to no avail.

"For my own good" Charlie sarcastically scoffed pulling a grey T-shirt over his rather pale and gaunt frame. "Tell me Dr Patel, what's the worst that can happen to me now?" he continued getting more and more agitated with every syllable. "You have just told me that I am going to die…but I can assure you that it won't be in one of these places" he concluded pulling on his American styled sneakers and reaching for his charcoal coloured bikers jacket, he had a steely certainty and was adamant.

"Ok…Ok" Dr Patel conceded, knowing nothing she could say would change Charlie's mind. "Will you at least wait a little longer so I can prepare your prescription?" she tried to barter. "If you won't stay in the hospital then you will need pain relief and further medication to both control your symptoms and make you comfortable"

Charlie thought for a moment before seeing that Dr Patel's argument made sense, begrudgingly he took a seat back on the bed. "Ok" he nodded the anger that once raged within him had begun to ease a little leaving Charlie a little out of breath and his heart beating a lot quicker than it normally did. "Half an hour and then I'm gone".

## Chapter Three.

With a navy travel bag in one hand and a white plastic bag containing a dozen or so boxes of medication in the other, the boxes containing different quantities and strengths to tackle the different regions of his illness, Charlie waited outside the hospital.

Standing beside a small group of chain smoking visitors Charlie couldn't resist inhaling the second hand smoke, he'd given up smoking a few years before and hadn't missed it until now, now he really wanted a cigarette.

About to ask for one from an elderly gentleman Charlie was haltered by the sounding of a car horn, turning to see Tommy pulled up beside him, looking a little harassed and flustered Tommy had received a phone call from the hospital to pick up Charlie, he'd raced there as quick as he could and leaving work to do so.

"Hey" he called beckoning to Charlie whilst gesturing out of the window with his hand.

Climbing in to the blue V.W Golf and throwing his bags on the back seat they set off in to the busy midday central London traffic, the March weather was glum and wet and yet it suited Charlie's mood perfectly.

"So how are you feeling?" Tommy asked, pulling free the red tie from his collar and throwing it on the back seat before unbuttoning the top button of his shirt.

"Good" Charlie quietly replied he wasn't in the mood to converse he just wanted to get home, to close out the world and be alone.

"So what did the consultant say?" Tommy asked another question knowing something wasn't right with how Charlie was acting, his entire demeanour was that of a stranger to him.

"She said I'd be fine in a few weeks as long as I keep taking the medication they've given me" Charlie lied a well rehearsed lie, spoken with enough conviction that it sounded believable.

"Well that's good…right?" smiled Tommy looking from the road to see the dull and rigid expression Charlie was exhibiting.

"Yeah" he returned with a singular reply whilst resting his head against the window, watching the city and its inhabitants hurriedly going about their daily routines.

Charlie's mind was a blackened blur, exhausted in its attempts to comprehend the premature death sentence that had been opposed upon him. "Why me?" he thought to himself, what had he done so wrong to deserve such a terrifying end, unfair was an understatement and thinking about it only aided in angering him further.

With the midday traffic being kind for once they soon reached the car park to Charlie's private apartment by the river. "Thanks for the lift" he faked a smile whilst grabbing his bags and opening the door.

"Wait" called Tommy his voice raised slightly but with an undertone of concern. "Are you sure you're alright mate?" he asked, his frowned expression gave him a saddened appearance.

"Yes, I'm fine" Charlie lied again with a scoff. "I'm just tired and want my own bed" he tried to sound as reassured as he could in his reply before exiting the car and closing the door.

"Oh…" called Tommy once more, remembering something he had needed to say as Charlie poked his head back in to the car window. "I forgot to tell you, when you were in the hospital you received a phone call from a storage company, they said your grandmother had rented a unit from them before going in to the nursing home" Tommy explained as Charlie looked back at him a little baffled, his grandmother had passed away the year before but she hadn't mentioned anything to him about any storage unit.

"They said the contract had ended and if you didn't collect the contents they were going to send to auction what they could sell and destroy the rest…so me and Lydia picked them up but didn't know where to put them, so we left them at your place" he concluded with a shrug.

"Ok, I'll sort it" Charlie nodded not really paying attention to something that he saw as far too trivial to worry about.

Turning the key in the lock and sliding across the chain Charlie secured his door, closing out the world beyond as he dropped his bags in the hallway and entered the living room, lowering himself on to his black leather sofa he sat in silence looking at the dozen or so towers each comprised of five cardboard storage boxes that stood around his black, chrome and cream minimalistic furnishings. The boxes contained mostly old trinkets and paperwork, it was all that was left of his grandmothers memory, of the women who had raised him since his mothers death.

For days Charlie hardly moved from the sofa his feelings of anger and bereavement were all consuming leaving nothing but a blackened void within, he didn't sleep nor eat and the furthest he ventured was to the bathroom and the kitchen to remove another bottle of vodka from his tall silver doubled door refrigerator, the alcohol served its purpose in dulling his thoughts and senses somewhat. The thought of not having a plan or a way to stop the inevitable of what was going to happen to him drove Charlie almost to madness, being out of control was something he couldn't handle, he'd lived his life with a strict plan already laid out in front of him, he'd wanted to go to university and then to work in the publishing business, from there he had hoped to run his own company representing international bestsellers that would in turn bring him success, the plan he had forged since being a teenager was now a future Charlie knew was never going to happen. Feeling saddened and scared and with the alcohol only further fuelling Charlie's dark emotions he had fallen in to a depressive and fragile state, not answering the door nor replying to the countless texts and e-mails that were marked as urgent Charlie had shut everyone out the best he could as him mind only descended further in to depression and despair.

The days turned in to weeks and no matter how hard Tommy and Lydia tried to see Charlie or get him to open the door Charlie wouldn't, telling them to go away and leave him alone. Knowing something was seriously wrong their worry for him intensified and even though they couldn't get to see him it didn't stop them from trying to help in any way they could, they began leaving food parcels of homemade meals and essentials such as bread, milk and toilet paper on his doorstep, their main concern was his health with him not long since leaving hospital.

Charlie had started on a road to destruction, he was unkempt, unwashed and very rarely changed his clothes, managing to snatch one or two hours a night before the drinking of his extensive and expensive alcohol collection began again, he had become lost within himself unable to find meaning in anything, he simply didn't care anymore.

Failing to take his medication prescribed by Dr Patel, Charlie's symptoms had already become more prominent and swiftly worsened with nothing in his system to fight back against the illness, tremors in his hands and upper arms were now a regular occurrence as were the almost unbearable headaches and migraines that plagued him like a hot lance penetrating his skull, jabbing back and fourth in to his flesh repeatedly, but in a rather perverse way Charlie didn't mind because if he could still feel pain to him that meant he was still alive.

Several loud raps struck his door accompanied with the constant buzzing of someone's finger being held down on the door bell, it was Lydia and she'd had enough, once realising that the banging and buzzing wasn't working she began to shout.

"Charlie, open this door" she ordered. "I'm not going anywhere until you do, so open up you selfish bastard" she continued whilst continuing to beat her hands against the door. Lydia was a naturally fiery and feisty personality, she was an East London girl who knew who she was and comfortable in her own skin, boisterous and heavy handed she didn't suffer fools gladly and even though she had known Charlie for over a decade and saw him almost like a brother Lydia wasn't going to pull any punches.

Eventually her persistence and tenacity paid off as she heard the releasing of the top bolt and the metallic sound of the chain sliding free, bursting through the door Lydia was hyper aggressive and ready for an argument, pulling down the hood of her red and grey fur collared coat she slammed the door behind her.

"What do you want?" Charlie groaned uninterested by Lydia's arrival as he propped himself up against the wall, his legs not able to keep him stable and upright unaided.

"You look terrible" she remarked taking off her coat as the close and humid atmosphere bereaved of fresh air that the apartment yielded delivered a stifling quality. "What are you doing to yourself?" she continued with a disappointing and disapproving expression fixed upon her face. Charlie's appearance worried her far more than she cared to admit the almost malnourished and ghostly pale sight before her was not the Charlie she knew, he'd always been clean shaven, his clothes always crisply pressed and he was never without a scent of expensive aftershave and expertly cropped hair, she didn't know the person before her.

"Is that it?" Charlie slurred his words slightly the alcohol that circulated his system had given him a new found and harshly critical confidence.

"No that isn't it, you selfish sod" she snapped. "We've been worried sick about you and you're in here drinking your body weight in booze…Tommy thought something serious had happened" she continued pushing passed him and heading in to the living room that looked dusty and filthy with half empty beer and vodka bottles casually laying all over the floor complete with a musty scent that seemed to stick inside her nostrils.

"Well now you've seen me you can tell Tommy that I'm fine…now just go and leave me alone" Charlie instructed whilst retaking his seat on the sofa and reaching for the nearest bottle.

"That's all he gets…your closest friend, my husband?" she spat back with a furious venom. "Do you know he's spent the last few weeks so worried about you that he's made himself ill" Lydia stood over him her hands flush to her hips whilst she waited for his riposte but it didn't come, Charlie deciding instead to take another gulp from the clear glass bottle.

Beginning to calm a little Lydia tentatively took a seat beside him. "What's going on Charlie, we know there's something you're not telling us?" she probed, her voice becoming more delicate and feminine. "This isn't you…none of this, just tell me what's going on".

Noticing a stream of tears rolling down his cheeks before Charlie began to slowly shake his head. "It's ok…it's me, you can talk to me about anything" she soothed clutching his forearm.

Lydia's contact made Charlie leap to his feet still holding the bottle he wiped away the tears with his sleeve whilst snorting loudly. "No…I think you should go".

"No" Lydia protested loudly she too getting to her feet. "I'm not going anywhere, not until you tell me what the hell is going on?".

Suddenly Charlie exploded in a mixture of anger, grief and frustration, throwing the bottle in to the fireplace and kicking over one of the towers of boxes, causing the contents of old papers and letters to spread across the laminated floor. "You want to know?" he boomed almost snarling. "I'm dying alright…I'm dying" he continued his voice losing volume and pitch part the way through his admission.

Speechless and dumbfounded by his revelation Lydia finally found her voice. "You're what?" she muttered hoping she had heard him wrong.

"I'm dying" he slowly repeated, his body tense and yet fragile as if like jelly inside. "I lied to you and Tommy when I said I was fine" he continued. "The truth is I have a brain tumour…a cancerous tumour that's inoperable".

Taking a hold of Charlie and hugging him as tight as she could Lydia's natural protective instincts immediately taking hold. "I'm so sorry" she gasped quietly a feeling of guilt was rife in her mind for how she had acted before, whilst a wave of fear and instant grief flowed freely throughout her body.

"Right" she spoke trying to gather herself. "You go and have a shower and a shave" she ordered her silent tears had destroyed her make up, Lydia's vulnerable side was a side of her that she didn't reveal willingly but she couldn't hold it back. "And I'll put the kettle on".

This time Charlie didn't argue and did what was asked of him whilst Lydia began a quick tidy round his apartment but once knowing she was alone she couldn't contain herself any longer, squatting on the floor she silently sobbed, feeling as if she was falling apart with the thought of losing Charlie and of how heartbroken Tommy was going to be once he heard the truth of what was happening to his best friend.

Pulling herself together as Charlie returned looking a little more like his old self Lydia and Charlie began to talk, she listened intently to what had happened over the past week from the diagnosis to Charlie's fears and frustrations, offering comfort when she could as well as being a shoulder to cry on as he wept and spoke of just how terrified he was of dying.

The hours of talking had left Charlie feeling drained and yet he felt an almost cathartic sensation and a relief that someone else now knew what he was going through and most important to him he now knew he wouldn't be facing what was to come alone.

"Thank you" Charlie smiled opening the front door as Lydia fastened the buttons of her coat.

"That's what I'm here for" she smiled back, giving him a hug and a peck on the cheek. "From now on you don't hide anything…you're not on your own in this" she instructed her finger pointed towards Charlie's chest as he nodded in agreement. "And if you need anything Tommy and I are only a phone call away".

Charlie's eyes widened and a sick feeling emanated from his stomach as a thought entered his head. "Oh God…I have to tell Tommy" he gasped knowing just how difficult that conversation was going to be, Tommy wasn't as strong mentally as Lydia and Charlie knew he would fall to pieces once hearing that the cancer had returned after all these years.

"I'll tell him" Lydia interjected seeing the pained look in Charlie's eyes by the mere thought of breaking it to Tommy. "I'll break it to him gently" she reassured with a rye and sympathetic smile as she headed out of the door.

Closing the door Charlie released a deep yet controlled breath feeling as though his eyes had finally reopened for the first time since he'd received the news of his terminal condition, he could see beyond the dark despair that had once obstructed and it was all thanks to Lydia. Emptying the few open bottles of vodka, wine and beer down the sink Charlie continued what Lydia had started and tidied up his apartment immediately ashamed that he had let it get to something that resembled a pig sty, once complete in his task he began moving the storage boxes that littered his living room a few at a time to the spare bedroom until he had only one overturned box remaining.

Packing up the correspondents, trinkets and photographs of his past Charlie came across a bundle of letters, letters in several different coloured envelopes and bound in brown string. Examining them closer he noticed they were all addressed to his mother Isabelle but more interestingly each one was unopened. A little intrigued Charlie pulled free the string to investigate them further, seeing each had several American postal marks stamped upon them for the transatlantic delivery to England whilst on the back there was a forwarding address to Lamont California if undelivered to a man named Robert Halliday.

Pricking Charlie's curiosity he couldn't help himself so carefully he opened one of the letters to see inside were two folded pages of paper, examining them further he read the unknown authors words as he professed love for Isabelle and how sorry he was that he had to return to America to be with his family. Charlie opened another that spoke of how the author couldn't stop thinking of his mother and how much he loved her despite the age gap between them, taking it upon himself Charlie opened the others reading them in turn to see that each of the letters followed the same theme of a besotted lover trying to make contact.

Following the dates that were etched in the top right hand corner of every correspondent he was able to place them in chronological order, the final letter was dated the 2nd of November 1988 making Charlie a little over two years old when it was written but the date resonated deeper within him as Charlie knew his mother had died in the September of that year. The letter spoke of how heartbroken the author was that Isabelle hadn't responded to any of their letters and that this would be their final attempt to contact her and if they received no response then they would have their answer and would not bother her again, signing off with. "I will love you until I draw my final breath and I wish you all of the happiness that you truly deserve. Robert X"

Charlie was captivated he knew very little about his mother with her passing when he was so young, the only information he could glean about her was through his grandmother, whom he had always thought was exceptionally careful with what she had told him, all he knew for certain was that Isabelle was fiercely intelligent and rather beautiful judging by the few photographs he had in his possession also that she had fallen pregnant with him after a one night stand and had to drop out of university to care for him, which she did up until her untimely demise two days before her 23rd birthday due to an undiagnosed heart condition.

Consumed by the mystery and intrigue that the letters had brought him Charlie was happy to have something other than his illness to think about, once finding a project he became instinctively anal and gregarious on the subject, he would become impassioned by it and would want to see it through to its end, and now he had the perfect project to do just that, a project that would occupy his mind that was severely malnourished in stimulus.

Hour upon hour passed well in to the early morning but Charlie couldn't stop himself from reading and rereading the letters a dozen or so times from the unknown American who seemed to truly love his mother, feeling invigorated for the first time in weeks almost excitable with an unrelenting appetite to find as much information as he could, ransacking the once neatly stacked storage boxes for anything that belonged to his mother, for anything that would aid him in his quest for answers. Finding her old textbooks and notepads from university none were much help except for two sets of initials scrawled on the inner pages that seemed to frequently appear, the first were (I M) his mothers and the others were (R H), Charlie believed they belonged to the mysterious American. Searching another box Charlie hit the jackpot finding a treasure trove of his late mothers possessions, beneath the dusty folded posters of an old rock band from the eighties and a dozen or so school reports he had found a series of journals, each of the covers brightly decorated with glitter and homemade stickers of flowers, the first journal started when she had just started secondary school.

Sensing his task would be more difficult than he first thought in finding what he was looking for Charlie was pleasantly surprised to find Isabelle was just as fastidious as he, writing the corresponding date at the top of the page before she made an entry, soon enough he found the right ones. Filing through her final two books that charted her thoughts, beliefs, dreams and fears as she turned sixteen leading all the way to her final few entries, the last few months of her writing seemed to be focused on one subject, the mysterious (R H) she wrote about how she thought she was falling in love with him and that she feared that he didn't even notice her.

"He spoke to me today" she wrote. "His smile melts me to my seat".

Charlie hurriedly read on, he was gripped consuming the words as if it was timeless classic, wanting to know what happened next he skipped a few pages to one where their relationship was in the height of its passion.

"When Robert kisses and holds me I feel safe, safer than I have ever felt before… knowing he has a wife and children makes me feel disgusted but I just can't stop myself, I love him so much"

Charlie was a little shocked by his mother's admission on actively entering in to an affair, however reading on he noticed her final few entries in her journal had become more solemn and rather darker.

"Robert has told me he has to go back to America and he doesn't know if he'll be able to come back to England, I don't know what I'm going to do"

But it was Isabelle's final entry that really affected Charlie, it was rife with despair and grief, the way she wrote gave him a sense of the pain she was experiencing.

"He left me today, I WANT TO DIE, my life is empty and bereaved of the happiness and joy that Robert seemed to exude…I don't think I will ever be able to love again, maybe if I had told him he'd have stayed…but it doesn't matter now, nothing matters to me anymore. And now I have to tell my mother about the predicament I've gotten myself in…MY LIFE IS OVER".

Closing the cover he reflected on what he'd read and as enthralling as it had been to glimpse in to a life he had never know about Charlie couldn't help but feel saddened for his mother knowing that three years after her heart was broken she was dead. Feeling as if he had found a connection he'd longed to have known by reading her journals Charlie had learned something about Isabelle as a person and not just snippets and selected information from the recollection of others.

Suddenly a question entered his head, something that had struck him as rather odd. "If my mother loved the American that much why didn't she reply to his letters" he asked himself out loud when he remembered something. "The letters were never opened…because she never received them" Charlie answered his own question whilst beginning to pace the living room as if addressing a jury in a court of law. "They'd been delivered but someone had gotten to them first" he assumed, knowing only one person would take it upon themselves to do such a thing, his grandmother. Charlie knew how fiercely loyal and protective his grandmother was and she may have sort to shield her daughter from any emotional harm but on the other hand she was tough and rarely forgiving and as the matriarch of the Marshall household her word was law, spiteful and hardened to respectability she could have seen her daughters affair with a married man as the ultimate stain of embarrassment upon the family name, sadly for Charlie he knew the latter was more plausible.

Lying in bed for the first time in a long while Charlie's body was relieved at its ability to relax but his mind shared no such luxury, tossing and turning and trying several different positions Charlie still couldn't sleep, his mind sparked with an unrelenting energy and vigour from everything he'd learned but yet one question still lingered.
"What predicament had she gotten herself in to?" he asked himself, quoting form Isabelle's journal.
"What could have been so bad that she was so terrified to tell her own mother?" he continued when the answer struck him like a slap to his face. "She was pregnant with me" he gasped sitting upright, his skin felt icy cool and ripe with goose bumps.
Charlie trembled as the revelation unfolded in his head as a feeling of both excitement and trepidation that fuelled his thoughts and theories, never knowing anything about his father not even his name Charlie had always been told he was the result of a one night stand where his mothers judgement was jaded by alcohol and the man was a fellow student who transferred to another university upon hearing the results of their actions.
Knowing his grandmothers tendency to bend the truth for her own ends Charlie knew there could be more than a possibility that she'd lied to him about his paternal lineage through the years of him growing up.
Wide awake and without the possibilities of him sleeping he pulled a T-shirt over his head and made himself a coffee before sitting down at his circular glass dining table armed with the letters, journals and his laptop.
Coagulating the dates from Isabelle's final entry in her journal to the date he was born matching them almost to nine months and doing so giving Charlie a sense of vindication that he could be right, Robert could be his father.
The decades of wondering who he was and where he had come from on his paternal side had left Charlie with a redundant frustration but now he had a name and a suspicious mind and that was all he needed. Using the name on the back of the envelope Charlie rapped the plastic keys of his laptop with a frantic energy as he researched the name Robert Halliday, in an instant hundreds of results stared back at him through the black and silver framed screen. Adding the university Isabelle attended in to the search engine the results narrowed down to a more amiable twenty nine but by the dates and the years that corresponded to Isabelle's attendance only left one result remaining.
With a burst of trepidation and nervousness running swiftly through his veins with the prospect of

what he was about to find, Charlie clicked on the link that referred his search to the universities history page that listed academic events.

"Robert Francis Halliday born the 12th November 1950, special guest lecturer summer 1988" he read aloud the result shocking Charlie, Robert was a lecturer and in his mid thirties, not the student he'd been led to believe.

The page told him that Robert was a celebrated historian and European literary expert and despite being a resounding hit with the students he had never returned to England to teach again. Wanting to know more about Roberts life both private and academically Charlie ciphered down the page and clicking on the biography link hoping it would yield more information. The biography revealed Robert was born in New Jersey in 1950, he had attended Harvard and earned himself a masters degree before embarking on a career in teaching, starting in a handful of high schools across the country before heading to Yale and finally back to Harvard where Robert had taken the position of history professor before briefly mentioning his short stay in England.

Reaching the personal part of his biography Charlie saw it, something that made all of the pieces of his mysterious departure fall in to place, Robert wasn't only married he had three young children too, maybe he had left Isabelle not to return to his wife but for the sake of his children thought Charlie hoping to form some sort of adequate excuse from Robert having to leave in his head, conceding to himself that he was probably wrong and would never get the real reason.

Married with three children but by 1993 Robert was divorced and never remarried or had any more children that his biographer knew of, nothing else was documented about his personal life and in fact not much more was documented about his career moves either, Robert had returned to Harvard and taught for a few years…then nothing, the final sentence on the page was a final update, dated from 2010 and stating Robert had retired and resided in Lamont California.

Charlie continued to search but couldn't find anything on Robert Halliday from the mid nineties up to his retirement, it had been as if he had simply vanished for fifteen years before re-emerging in 2010 and promptly retiring. With nothing left to read Charlie sat back in his chair removing his glasses to rub his sore feeling eyes with one question still whirring at the forefront of his mind, just who was Robert Halliday.

## Chapter Four

Queuing for a coffee in a café not too far from his apartment Charlie waited for Tommy and Lydia, he had arranged for them to meet him there for the first time since he had told Lydia of his illness and Charlie knew exactly what to expect.

The small humid café bustled in the lunchtime rush with people requiring their caffeine fix and a sandwich of something more hearty and warm whilst on their lunch breaks. After collecting his change Charlie looked for a table but as he turned he saw Tommy and Lydia in the doorway, Tommy's eyes looked red and swollen as if he had been crying all night and was ready to restart at any moment.

Wading through the crowd to reach Charlie they embraced in an air defying bear hug, Charlie remained as still as he could in an attempt to not spill his freshly prepared coffee whilst Tommy's body twitched and convulsed a little as he silently wept. "I'm sorry mate" he managed to say with a struggle.

"I know…I know" Charlie replied lightly patting him on the back in an attempt to comfort Tommy even though it was him who was ill and suffering.

Tommy had always been the more sensitive and emotional of the two, anything could tug at his heart strings no matter how small or seemingly insignificant whether it was pictures of new born babies or a romantic film he always cried, Charlie on the other hand was rather stunted and impotent in that department he had trouble showing even the smallest tinge of emotion which in turn gave him a rather cold demeanour, he'd always bottled things up which inevitably shut everyone out.

Holding him a little too long for Charlie's liking and with several customers in the café giving them some confused, perturbed glances and stares Lydia helped him to break free. They headed for a recently vacated table as a young teenage waitress hurriedly removed empty plates and cups before wiping down the waterproof table protector for them to use.

"Whatever the doctor said, we can get a second opinion…we can find a different specialist" offered Tommy, forever the optimist as he sort to find a solution for Charlie's plight.

Charlie slowly shook his head. "There's nothing that can be done Tommy, no matter how many different doctors or specialists I see it wont change the facts…the tumour in my head is inoperable" he shrugged a little deflated but Charlie was slowly coming to terms with what was approaching in his very near future. "All the doctors can do is prescribe medication to help with the pain" he concluded sipping at his sweet and still steaming beverage. Unable to keep any prolonged eye contact with his best friend, he glanced outside at the people walking passed the condensation riddled window pretending to be a lot more interested than he really was.

Tommy's lip quivered as Lydia held and lightly squeezed his hand in reassurance, once hearing that there wasn't anything he could do to prevent what was happening to Charlie the realisation of him dying immediately began to wreak havoc within him. "How long have they given …" he stopped himself unable to continue asking the question whilst his body trembled.

"I have six months…a year, if I'm lucky" he responded rather clinically. "If I'm lucky" Charlie scoffed taking another drink from his cup, the one thing he knew he didn't have was luck.

Tommy looked broken his optimistic spark on life and naturally sunny disposition had deserted him. The atmosphere descended in to a dark silence the sort of tense atmosphere that you could cut with a knife, leaving his body ravished of everything Tommy felt hollow and empty.

Noticing the bunch of bound envelopes sitting on top of Charlie's bag Lydia saw her chance to try and alleviate the almost claustrophobic silence and change the subject that was stifling them. "What's with the letters?"

Lydia's question delivered the perfect distraction as Charlie readily explained what he had found in the letters and the journals as well as online while allowing Lydia to look through the letters he produced a brown A4 sized folder containing his freshly printed research on Robert, his vigour and optimism on the subject was a little surprising for his friends.

"Wait…hold on" spoke Lydia finding it difficult to keep up with the excitability of Charlie whilst he presented the information, she couldn't understand why he had become so invested on events that had taken place thirty years in the past. "Where are you going with this Charlie?" she asked. Charlie took a moment looking between the confused expressions of his friends. "I think this Robert Halliday…I think he could be my dad".

Charlie's statement immediately rocked them, neither could have imagined that this was going to be his explanation and so Lydia and Tommy's mirrored expressions transformed from one of confusion to one of wide eyed bewilderment. Whilst sharing glances with one another neither knew how to respond but the enthusiasm that oozed from Charlie drew them in like a moth to a flame. Explaining and highlighting the evidence he had provided and drawing on the fact that he had never known his father nor been told who he was as well as the dates in his mother's journals, Charlie concurred that the only male she had even mentioned was the American lecturer, the only man she had a relationship with during the timeline of his conception.

"Wow" exhaled Tommy staring a little aghast. "You really think this bloke could be your dad mate?" Tommy knew how difficult it had been for Charlie being raised by his grandparents he'd always told him how jealous he was of the paternal relationship that Tommy had always taken for granted.

"I think he could be" Charlie answered with a rye yet hopeful smile, he hoped he wasn't going mad and that Tommy and Lydia could see the rather high probability in his findings as he did.

"So what are you going to do?" asked Lydia still processing the information but never the less she couldn't hide her intrigue and shared a little of Charlie's confidence, though she didn't want to admit it just yet, she wanted to be methodical with her thoughts before voicing her final opinion.

"I don't know?" Charlie answered with a shrug of the shoulders and he was being truthful, in all of his excitement in finding the treasure trove of information he hadn't even begun to think about what he was going to do with it at all.

Once back home Charlie was greeted by a parcel waiting for him on the doorstep, pulling off the wrapping to find it was a book he'd ordered online, a book written by Robert Halliday, it was something about 17th century German literature although it wasn't the subject that Charlie was interested in but the picture of the author on the back of the blurb. Turning over the four hundred paged hardback Charlie was about to see for the first time what Robert Halliday looked like. A black and white portfolio picture stared back at him of a man short in stature yet stout and with a proud and prominent chin and nose, well groomed, bright smiled and eyes that yielded a rather intriguing and mysterious quality.

"So you're Robert Halliday?" he spoke out loud whilst looking intently at the blurb on the jacket cover, trying to find any similarities or characteristics they shared but no matter how long he stared at the image before him Charlie couldn't be sure.

Sitting at the dining table after finishing his meal for one and digesting the several capsules of medication he'd been instructed to take, Charlie gazed out at the London skyline by moonlight, a view he never tired of seeing. The question that Lydia had asked him left Charlie in somewhat of a quandary, still unable to answer what he was going to do with the information he'd acquired, he had always swayed on the side of caution in everything he had done throughout his life never taking any unnecessary chances, but whilst looking out upon the illuminated city Charlie came to a decision. It was rash, radical and uncharacteristic for Charlie but he realised he had nothing to lose and next to no time for anymore regrets so he knew he had to be spontaneous for once and throw caution to the wind.

Turning on his laptop he immediately directed himself to the Heathrow airports website, hurriedly Charlie scanned the list of destinations with his fingers rapping swiftly across the keys and quickly he found a flight out of London to Bakersfield California that departed in four days' time. Knowing he couldn't stop because if he did he may back out of the impulsive decision altogether, Charlie confirmed his purchase before having the chance to lose his nerve and almost immediately receiving an E-mail of confirmation of his booking.

Feeling a sudden surge of exhilaration ride up within him Charlie closed his laptop his fingers drumming repeatedly against its plastic top as he hoped he'd made the right decision, but deep down Charlie knew he had to follow his instincts and they were telling him that he needed to seek the truth to find his paternal heritage.

With his medication restocked, a small wheeled suitcase packed and his trusty satchel over his shoulder Charlie was ready to go, locking up his apartment he headed downstairs. His mind was a mixture of nervousness and doubt that threatened to overthrow his reasoning, the thoughts Charlie knew he couldn't afford to let in.

"Are you ready?" asked Lydia, she and Tommy had agreed to drive him to the airport.

"As I'll ever be" Charlie replied as Tommy took his case and placed it in the boot.

"I have to ask, are you sure you're doing the right thing mate?" Tommy hesitantly asked the question receiving a sharp look from his wife. "I just don't want you to get hurt" he explained daring himself to continue and soon enough his courage gathered momentum. "Ok let's play devil's advocate for a minute and say you travel half the way around the world to meet this bloke and he doesn't want anything to do with you".

Charlie stood silent for a second or two as the thought had already crossed his mind more than once or twice. "Then I'll have to deal with it but at least I know that I've tried".

Setting off with plenty of time to spare and taking the busy central traffic of the nonstop city in to consideration Charlie sat quietly while his stomach felt as if it was doing somersaults, Lydia and Tommy felt incredibly sad and a little deflated with Charlie's imminent and rather impulsive departure, attempting to hide their true feelings behind the support and encouragement they offered to his decision.

The slow caravan of traffic led throughout the bustling city streets littered with double decker buses at every stop on their route whilst the black hackney cabs and their kamikaze drivers jostled for every space on the tarmac for every possible fare, making their progression slow and frustrating.

"Pull over here" ordered Charlie as the car passed the traffic lights on amber just before the offices of Doors and Handley.

"What…why?" asked Tommy making eye contact with Charlie via the rear view mirror. "We're running late as it is" he continued his fingers rapping against the steering wheel willing the cars in front to spontaneously disappear.

"There's something I have to do…I'll be two minutes" explained Charlie escaping the confines of the still slow moving car.

Hurrying along the pavement toward his work place Charlie saw Jason standing at the foot of the steps before its entrance, he was attempting to smoke a cigarette whilst a blustering wind seemed to whip between the tall standing buildings that acted like a vacuum.

"Hey" said Charlie grabbing Jason's attention who was a little surprised to see Charlie standing before him, the last time he'd seen him Charlie was unconscious at the presentation dinner.

"I thought you were on leave?" Jason spoke a little accusingly, his naturally untrusting nature sparked in his consciousness not really knowing what else to say, he and Charlie had rarely seen eye to eye and hadn't much in common except work. "So…how are you feeling?" Jason finally mustered a subject to converse about.

"Yeah, I'm fine" Charlie answered, he too feeling a little awkward. "I need you to do me a favour" he continued retrieving a rectangle shaped envelope from the inside pocket of his jacket and handing it to Jason. "I want you to give this to human resources".

His long tailed winter coat billowed in the breeze as Jason glared from Charlie and to the envelope and back again a little puzzled.

"What's this?" he asked as his perfectly quaffed hair was returned back in to place with his hand as the wind continued to wreak havoc.

"Its my resignation" Charlie answered him, watching as his words caused Jason to frown and his eyes to squint as three deep lines manifested upon his forehead. "So I guess the partnership is yours" Charlie continued.

"Why?" he replied rather sharp, he was stunned with what he was hearing and more than a little suspicious a feeling that at that moment seemed to sear through him.

"Because I've realised that there's more important things in life than work, money and success, and I haven't the time to keep putting the things I need to do off anymore" Charlie tried to explain but Jason's almost pained expression didn't offer any acknowledgement of comprehension as he did so. "I hope the job makes you happy, I really do because you deserve it". As Charlie spoke he was alerted by the sound of Tommy's car horn being rapidly pressed, reminding him of their now slight time frame.

Offering his hand Jason slowly took it and they shook firmly. "Just do me one thing…don't be so much of a dick" Charlie quipped with a smile.

"I'll try" Jason smiled back watching as Charlie hurriedly made his way back to the car, taking the last few drags of his cigarette before flicking it in to the gutter he headed excitedly back inside the office, feeling vindicated and as though all of his Christmas' had come at once, Jason couldn't wait to deliver the letter to his superiors.

Arriving at the airport with little time to spare Charlie prepared to say his goodbyes. "Well this is it" he smiled pulling up the retractable handle on his case.

"Have you got everything, passport, ticket, money?" Lydia asked making him show her he had everything, once satisfied she hugged him tightly. "I'm going to miss you" she whispered, her voice a little croaky as she willed herself to keep it together. "Go and find your dad Charlie, he's going to love you…I know he will" she reassured before kissing him on the cheek.

"Thank you" Charlie replied kissing her back, Lydia knew just what to say and when to say it to steady his nerves and she had done it again without even trying, she had managed to put Charlie at ease as his nerves were threatening to get the better of him.

Letting Charlie go Tommy took his wife's place, they hugged a manly hug with plenty of back slapping as dozens of people were entering and exiting the international airport, most looked hurried and harassed or excited with the prospect of the holiday to come and several people were exhaustedly trying to hail a cab after their long flights home to Britain.

"Be careful out there mate and remember you can call us anytime…we're here whenever you need us" Tommy instructed acting as if he and Lydia were his parents.

"I'll call you when I land" Charlie smiled as he began to walk away before suddenly stopping himself. "Oh…I almost forgot" he spoke whilst retrieving something from his pocket. "You'll need these" Charlie produced the keys to his apartment, throwing them to Tommy.

"I don't understand?" he returned a little startled whilst looking to Lydia who looked as baffled as he did.

"The apartments yours…to do with what you want, live in it, sell it, its up to you".

"But when you come back where are you going to live?" Tommy exclaimed as Lydia clutched his arm, she felt she already knew the answer to his question.

"I'm not coming back Tommy" Charlie returned his voice light yet quiet as he watched his speechless friends before him, their eyes had become immediately sunken and dull.

Everything they had tried to push from their minds had returned with a vengeance, all of their sadness they had managed to keep hidden was becoming ever visible with a shared raw and distraught expression. The grim reality of knowing Charlie wasn't going to return and the moments they now shared could very well be their last was becoming too much to bare and only aided in intensifying their gut wrenching heartbreak.

"But…" Tommy began but he was swiftly silenced.

"Please…don't, it'll be ok" Charlie interrupted feeling his voice trembling as he spoke. "Just be happy for me and look after each other" he continued offering a warm and comforting smile whilst receiving a slow nod of acceptance from Tommy whose body and posture had become slightly contorted whilst he pressed his fingers against his lips in a attempt to stop himself from crying. Taking a deep breath Charlie walked through the sliding automatic doors pulling his case behind him as he made his way towards the check in desk, looking back to wave one final time he tried to keep strong as he couldn't bear to see Tommy and Lydia looking so heartbroken especially knowing that he was the cause of it.

"Hey Charlie" called Tommy over the hundreds of travellers pacing the airport. "I'll see you soon". Charlie smiled back before reaching the check in desk, whispering under his breath. "No Tom…no you won't".

## Chapter Five

The automatic doors slid open allowing the intense heat of the California sun to hit Charlie, leaving the polished floors and air conditioning behind he ventured outside and immediately began to sweat. He removed his jacket and laid it over his satchel before fumbling for his prescription sunglasses, the heat was unbearable and he opted to stay beneath the flat roofed entrance whilst his fellow passengers mulled passed him, like Charlie they were tired after their long haul journey.

He took a moment to take in his new and alien surroundings whilst resetting his watch to local time, it was 11.30 am, Meadowfields international airport stood alone in the Bakersfield landscape the massive structure was both grand and aesthetically pleasing even coming from London where everything was architecturally beautiful and ripe with history whilst towering overhead was the norm Charlie was still impressed.

He headed out in to the midday sun looking for transport, watching as the other passengers were picked up by friends or family, their warm embraces signalled that they hadn't seen one other in a while. The passengers who didn't have loved ones to meet them headed for the car rental bureau almost marching in unison as they did so, dragging their luggage behind them.

Charlie on the other hand looked for the area reserved for taxi's a little away from the entrance but the parking ports were empty, Charlie had travelled through enough international airports to know that it was rather odd to see no eagerly awaiting weary travellers from recently landed flights. Seeing none on the horizon he resorted to plan B, public transport, following the designated signs to the bus stop he hoped for more luck. Finding the timetable on a tall rotating stand Charlie span it around with his hand seeing on either side that the times and destinations from Meadowfields airport were missing as he did so, the timetable had been replaced with a A4 size sign reading. 'All buses suspended from Friday 4th to Tuesday 8th due to striking action'. Charlie sighed in a defeatist manner, his forehead rested on the sign post, he was exhausted and irritable desperate to reach Lamont and find a hotel.

"Can I help you sir?" sounded a voice behind him.

Charlie turned to see a short and rather rotund African American man, wearing navy and grey overhauls and with an I.D badge attached to his breast pocket. "I see the buses are on strike" he began, receiving a confirming nod from the airport employee. "So is there any chance of finding a taxi?". Charlie asked hopefully.

"Unfortunately sir the taxi companies are on strike too" the man replied in a deep yet rich American tone, seeing the dejected expression on Charlie's face he decided to elaborate "Due to the ongoing talks between the mayors office and the drivers union the taxi companies decided to strike in support".

"Right…ok" Charlie answered resorting to plan C in his head. "Then can I rent a car?" he continued remembering dozen of his fellow passengers had headed towards the rental bureau whilst he foolishly dallied.

"Ah…" said the man his face scrunching slightly as Charlie braced himself, knowing by the man's expression that it wasn't going to be good news. "All the cars we had for rental have been reserved prior to your flight landing",

Charlie rubbed the back of his neck squeezing it a little in frustration, the other passengers must have known about the strike, the only one in the dark about it was seemingly him. "Then what am I supposed to do…I need to get to Lamont" he almost snapped whilst beginning to lose his patience.

"Lamont?" the man returned watching Charlie nod. "Lamont is twenty miles away, I don't think you'll be getting there today sir".

"Then do you have any suggestions?".

"You could walk…Bakersfield is only a few miles away, you'd be able to find somewhere to stay" he answered with the only suitable suggestion that he could think of.

"Walk" Charlie stated, looking down the seemingly endless highway in the direction the man was pointing, knowing there was no other option unless he slept in the airport for the next few days which was something Charlie was not going to do. "Right…I guess I'm walking, thank you for your help" he spoke his tone ripe with sarcasm.

Charlie began to walk pulling up the retractable handle on his travel case and pulling it behind him, leaving Meadowfields and taking to a small, dusty pathway beside the highway, the heat of the sun was almost unbearable it felt to Charlie as if it was at its most intense and severe as it beat down upon him relentlessly.

With a small yellow stoned rock face that trailed beside the highway to his right Charlie followed the baron track, feeling as if he had been walking for hours his progression slowed. The thought of hitchhiking crossed his mind but he'd seen very few vehicles and they had been travelling in the wrong direction on the almost deserted road, the vehicles he'd seen were large fuel trucks, their silver cylinders glistening in the sun and large lorries carrying their loads, beginning to feel weak, light headed and sick, Charlie was dehydrated and his body running low on meds.

Managing to produce enough saliva to choke down an oval shaped pill it felt like he was trying to swallow down a large stone or rock. After taking a short break and leaning upon the wooden frame of what he assumed used to be a fence, a small red 1977 Ford pickup truck with a dozen or so cardboard boxes in the back passed him, slowly it came to a stop indicating to Charlie for him to catch up with it.

Without a second thought Charlie did just that hurriedly dragging his case behind him, he didn't care who had stopped he just wanted to escape the blistering heat, reaching the truck a young women poked her head out of the open driver's window with a bright smile, the sort of smile that would have knocked anyone for six and Charlie was no exception.

"Hey…are you lost?" she beamed a naturally welcoming smile.

Charlie struggled to speak he was taken aback by the woman before him, she was petite and extraordinarily pretty, with brown hair that had a slight and natural curl, emerald green eyes and pale alabaster skin, Charlie thought her complexion looked a little out of place in the blisteringly sunny climate.

"I'm trying to get to Bakersfield" he finally managed to reply.

"You're English?" she asked her smile never faltering as Charlie nodded. "I've never met anyone from England before" she continued. "I'm heading in to the city…if you wanna ride?".

"Yeah…yes please, that would be great" he stumbled, immediately feeling awkward in his own skin, the sun felt at its hottest and his body felt as if it was reaching boiling point.

"Well alright…so are you gonna get in?" she gestured toward the passenger side door, she could sense the awkwardness and tried to quell it with her quirky deadpan sense of humour.

"Oh…yes…of course…sorry" said Charlie physically wanting to slap himself for acting like a bumbling idiot, he threw his case in the back.

Getting in they set off whilst the radio played low, so low that Charlie couldn't identify what song it was or who was singing it, the journey became quickly lost in a awkward silence with nothing but a few shared smiling glances between them. Charlie stole a look at his saviour who was wearing a red and white chequered shirt with the sleeves rolled up to the elbows and a white vest beneath it, light blue jeans and black heeled boots which added a little height to her 5'2 frame. Realising he was staring Charlie was afraid of seeming weird and so he deviated his gaze out on to the road ahead absorbing the idyllic view and even though he didn't want to admit it because of how corny it sounded in his head, the view resembled something out of a movie.

"I'm Jessie by the way" she introduced herself offering her free hand whilst still watching the road ahead.

"Charlie" he replied whilst shaking her hand, he couldn't understand what was the matter with him, he'd never been so nervous around a woman, behaving as if he'd never met one before and that he had been raised in a monastery never experiencing a woman's company.

"So Charlie, what brings you to America?...holiday?" she asked determined not to let the quiet take hold once more, Jessie was far more comfortable and confident than Charlie, she has long been accustomed to hiding her more vulnerable side beneath a toughened exterior.

"Sort of" he slowly replied. "I thought I'd come and check out California" he lied not feeling comfortable in revealing his true motive for being in California to a stranger, Jessie seemed a friendly stranger but a stranger never the less.

"Well alright" she smiled. "We don't get a lot of tourists around these parts, they normally head for the coast...you know for the sun, sea" she stopped herself from becoming too graphic. "Well you know what I mean".

Charlie threw her a knowing grin. "The whole LA experience has never really appealed to me".

"Really" she sounded surprised, most tourists to California lapped up the intoxicating allure of the Hollywood lifestyle where everything seemed possible and preconceptions that the streets were paved with gold. "Me neither, well I'm not the stereotypical tall blonde am I" she gestured up and down her petite brunette exterior with her hand.

"So what are your plans in Bakersfield?"

"Nothing" he shrugged. "I'm just going to find a hotel for the night and then try and get to Lamont in the morning" he answered as a breeze whipped through the cab of the truck bringing with it a brief relief from the humidity.

"Lamont?" she asked. "You're heading to Lamont?" she continued watching Charlie nod in confirmation. "Me to" Jessie grinned thinking it was fate that had urged her to stop and pick Charlie up, something she normally never did. "That's where I'm heading, I live in Lamont" she gestured flamboyantly as Charlie began to realise her overly theatrical movements when she spoke was a subconscious habit.

"I have to pick up a few things then I'm heading there...if you want to, you can come with me?" she offered.

"Really that would be great" Charlie replied not quite believing his luck, having such a bad start to his day since arriving at the airport, he thought he was due a bit of luck.

Reaching the busy and bustling city of Bakersfield, not too dissimilar to London in many ways it was a vast metropolis of large towering buildings and multicultural inhabitants going about their business, they pulled in to a Costco where Jessie's order was already waiting by the service exit for her to pick up. Another dozen boxes that Charlie helped load in to the back of the truck before they headed back on to the highway and as time wore on they began to warm to one another's company, enough so for Charlie to become more comfortable in his surroundings and begin to come out of his shell a little more.

"So what part of England are you from?" Jessie asked wanting to keep the free flowing conversation going.

"London" he replied without hesitation.

"Seriously?" she gasped looking to Charlie as he nodded. "I've always wanted to visit London, I always dreamt of going and spending a few years there, just to take in the history, the culture, oh my god the literature from England is the best" she gushed excitedly whilst thinking how incredibly lucky Charlie was for living there with such a rich tapestry at his fingertips.

"It's beautiful, especially in winter" smiled Charlie with the thought of home flashing immediately in his mind. "Why haven't you been?"

"Well, you know, bad timing…money" she shrugged as they passed a tall sign welcoming them to Lamont.

Lamont looked almost deserted compared to the big city beside it, it was quiet and looked at first glance as if it would be a rather nice and peaceful place to live, with a population of only twenty thousand there was little wonder of why the streets looked quieter.

"You're a long time dead" said Charlie, his eyes devouring his new surroundings whilst he spoke.

"One day I'll go" Jessie was rather insistent, she had made herself the promise that she would escape the small town and see the world a thousand times before but she had never had the courage to act upon it.

"Time passes without you realising…then before you know it you've ran out and trust me I know how that feels" he stated still looking out of the window, the lack of time he had and the debilitating effect caused by his illness was constantly on Charlie's mind, the worry and the fear never really left his thoughts for too long.

Charlie's words had brought the atmosphere down somewhat with Jessie not quite knowing what to make of his statement but she knew her questioning on the subject would have to wait as she pulled off the main road and in to the rear car park of a diner.

Pulling the stick shift beside the steering wheel in to park and turning off the engine they were greeted by the sight of a huge twenty stone man lurching towards them. He was as big in stature as in weight and of Hawaiian decent, wearing a bright blue flowery shirt unbuttoned to show a discoloured T-shirt beneath it whilst a white apron with the words 'Dino's Diner' written across it in red covered his shorts. The slaps of his flip flops drew closer as he reached the rear of the truck, he was a man mountain almost casting a full shadow over Charlie's five foot seven inched frame.

"You're late" he grunted. "And who's this?" he asked looking from Jessie to Charlie who immediately felt uncomfortable.

"Traffic" Jessie over emphasised with her arms aloft whilst she shrugged. "This is Charlie…he's from England" she beamed showing Charlie off like he was a new exhibit at a museum. "This is Caesar, he owns the diner".

"Good to meet you" Caesar boomed with a deep masculine tone, his hand not too dissimilar in size to a boxing glove engulfed Charlie's as they shook.

"And you" he tried not to wince through the vice like grip.

"Here's just landed" Jessie interjected watching the two men exchange welcoming pleasantries.

"Is that right" Caesar returned a little unimpressed to say the least. "Welcome to America" he spoke turning his attention back to Jessie. "The dinner rush has just started, I need you to run the floor".

"Eh, eh…ok fine" she sighed unable to find a good enough excuse to stay, almost stamping her foot like a petulant child. "You hungry Charlie?" she swiftly turned her frown back in to smile.

"Oh…no I think I'm going to find a hotel" he gestured pointing over his shoulder back toward the main road.

"What". She stated rather sharply, surprising herself with how reluctant she was to see Charlie leave. "You can't leave" she almost yelped, gathering some composure she started again. "You can't come all the way to Lamont and not eat at Dino's".

Caesar agreed instantly with a heavy nod forwards he took great pride in the food that he called his creation using the secrets given to him by his father who started the restaurant.

"Come on, it's my treat…as a thank you for helping me out with the boxes".

Charlie was struggling to say no to the hopeful and angelic face of Jessie. "Well…how can I say no to such a kind offer" he relented with a smile rubbing the back of his head that had been aching for a while but now it had begun to throb as Jessie took his arm in hers and began to guide him towards the rear door of the restaurant.

"Hey London" called Caesar causing Charlie to stop dead in is tracks, he slowly turned around. "There's no such thing as a free meal…are you gonna give me a hand?"

"Oh…of course, sorry" said Charlie heading back toward the truck.

"I'll see you inside" Jessie called heading inside, putting her hair in to a tight ponytail as she did so.

Several trips of carrying two boxes at a time had rendered Charlie exhausted whilst Caesar had carried four at a time and hadn't broken a sweat. Propping himself up against the doorframe with one hand outstretched to steady himself, his body trembled inside as if in shock as Charlie began to realise just how severely the disease was beginning to affect him not just mentally but for the first time physically, and that terrified him.

"Hey, macho man" called Caesar dropping the boxes in the store room beside the kitchen seeing Charlie was struggling. "I'll take it from here".

"Are you sure?" he gasped still a little out of breath as beads of sweat from his forehead gathered at his eyebrows.

"Yeah, I got this" he insisted. "Go, get something to eat".

Caesar stomped back toward the truck his giant frame swayed from side to side as he did so, pulling two more boxes toward the edge of the tail gate he was bemused with what a little manual work had done to Charlie. "What do they feed them in England?" he scoffed aloud to himself whilst shaking his head in disbelief.

Charlie headed inside the pristine kitchen its air conditioning felt like heaven on his skin as he found himself in the middle of well organised chaos, the glistening steel grills were at full capacity with burgers, chicken and steaks whilst two deep fryers sizzled harmoniously all under the watchful eyes of two young cooks, each had been taught by Caesar. A dozen male and female severs hurriedly weaved between one another as they battled the lunchtime rush , the restaurant was alive with a multitude of sounds and noises from orders been barked, the hissing and spitting of the frying food and the pinging sound of the brass plated serving bell when an order was ready. He managed to pass the seemingly oblivious cooks and waiters as Jessie appeared through a swinging red door with several dirty plates clutched in her arms, she looked hot and flustered but still managed a smile for Charlie, dropping the plates beside the sink she wiped her hands on her apron and moved the loose hair from her ponytail that had fallen in her face, tucking it behind her ear.

"Hey, come with me" she instructed leading the way out of the kitchen and in to a large half moon shaped room with a large silver counter that stretched its length with stools fixed to the black and white chequered floor and spaced at regular intervals beside it.

The diner was a hive of activity, alive with forty or so hungry customers packed in to the ten booths of large circular red faux leather seating surrounding a single table, each easily seating six or more they were positioned by large windows overlooking Lamont's main commercial street, that housed twenty or so stores, a bakery a few boutiques and three bars lined either side of the road.

"Here" Jessie stopped beside the smallest booth they had, it was secluded in the corner making it rather intimate and almost hidden beside the counter. "What can I get you to drink?" she asked resting her thumbs in the top of her apron.

Charlie almost folded in his seat, sighing in relief as he did so. "Eh…" he stuttered unsure of the options. "Coffee…please".

"Regular, cappuccino, latte" Jessie began reeling off a well memorised inventory of beverages with her notepad at the ready.

"Just coffee" he smiled.

"Ok...I'll be right back" Jessie spirited away, behind the counter with a spring in her step.

Charlie began examining the laminated menu that was sat in the middle of the table beside a metallic napkin dispenser and multiple condiments as Jessie reappeared complete with a glass pot of black coffee, pouring it in to the awaiting cup before Charlie, who for him since giving up smoking coffee had become his biggest vice, taking in the aroma of the roasted beans it gave him a little twinge that resembled elation.

"Do you see anything you like?" she asked seeing the menu in his grasp.

"Not really' his reply soft as he didn't want to sound pompous or rude whilst he continued to peruse it. "Everything sounds good".

"I know what you need?" she smiled with a knowing nod. "You need the Dino special".

Bowled over by her enthusiasm of the product and the conviction in her voice Charlie agreed with a nod whilst trying to look as enthused as Jessie was with her suggestion even though he hadn't a clue what he had just ordered.

"One Dino special coming up" she jotted it down and hurried toward the kitchen.

Relaxing back in his seat whilst sipping his coffee Charlie managed with ease to drown out the chaos and noise of the lunchtime rush that surrounded him, he'd been travelling for close to twenty hours and sitting in the booth was the closest he had come to being comfortable and he wasn't going to waste it. Retrieving his brown folder and the envelopes from his satchel he looked over his notes on Robert as he had done countless times before, but this time was different he knew he was so close to both finding and meeting him, a burst of excitable energy surged through him like a shock of electricity, the sensation drew a slight smile across his thin lips.

"Refill?" came a familiar voice as a coffee pot entered his peripheral vision, drawing him out of his daydream.

"Err...please" Charlie offered his cup as his forearm cautiously rested over the papers in an attempt to obscure them from view.

Placing the pot on the table Jessie knelt on the seat before him resting her elbows on the table having become intrigued with what Charlie was seemingly trying to hide. "What's in the folder?" she asked bluntly, leaning in a little more she tried to sneak a peak, her curiosity getting the better of her.

"Oh…it's nothing" he replied hurriedly pushing the ten or so pages back in to the folder whilst becoming defensive.

"Is it work?" she asked again resting her chin on her hand.

Charlie shook his head. "No" as he pushed them back in his bag, sipping once again at his coffee whilst trying to act as normal as possible.

"I never asked, what you did for a job back home" Jessie spoke again her line of questioning showed no signs of ending, she was brimming with a nervous energy that invigorated her and it seemed to happen every time she was in Charlie's company, and she liked the way it made her feel.

"I'm an agent for a publishing company, I represent a few clients making sure they receive the best monetary deal for their work" he explained as Jessie became increasingly interested, once kneeling she quickly sat down her gaze intensely fixed on him.

"Who do you represent?" she asked excitedly. "Anyone I'd know?"

"Anthony James, Peter Fitzgerald, Bridget Gellar, Belinda Thomas"

"Shut up" Jessie gasped. "Belinda Thomas, the poet?" she asked as Charlie nodded a little surprised with her reaction of Charlie personally knowing her.

"I love her" she gasped. "She inspired me to write poetry".

"You're a writer?" he asked receiving an eager nod in response. "Well if you'd like I'd be more than happy to take a look at them" Charlie smiled helpfully offering his professional opinion on her work.

"No" she spoke sharp, declining the offer as gracefully as she could instantly feeling embarrassed. "It's just a hobby, they're not very good" she continued it was now her turn to become a little defensive and vulnerable.

The service bell began to ping frantically causing them both to turn their heads in the direction of where the sound was coming from seeing as they did so the huge frame of Caesar protruding through the service hatch. "Hey" he boomed. "I don't pay you to sit down with the customers Jessie".

With a deep exhale and a roll of the eyes Jessie got back to her feet. "Oh" she remembered something, reaching in to her pocket she retrieved a folded piece of paper. "Here's the address for a hotel, it's only a few blocks from here" she explained offering it to Charlie.

"Thank you…but you didn't have to go to any trouble" he replied taking the paper from her.

"Its no trouble the owner is a friend of mine, I've already phoned ahead and they're expecting you" she smiled lifting the coffee pot and stroking Charlie's shoulder as she walked away.

"Thank you…again" Charlie called over his shoulder, he thought it odd just how accommodating Jessie had been with him but being a stranger in even stranger surroundings Charlie wasn't going to turn down such a kind gesture.

The lunchtime rush began to ease and the diner had begun to quieten as Charlie relaxed in the somewhat private booth he watched the world go by out of the window when suddenly he felt a slight numbness in his left hand, looking down he saw it had begun trembling uncontrollably just like it had done at the office dinner. Beginning to perspire and a feeling of nausea engulfing his body Charlie tried to stand but immediately regretted his decision to do so as his vision blurred causing him to slump back in to his seat.

Petrified at what was happening to him Charlie tried to remain calm, clutching his hand he felt helpless and weak, not noticing his distress Jessie cleaned a now empty booth as a group of four men all in their late twenties burst through the door shouting and laughing and with a few beers already consumed they were in a rowdy mood.

The leader of the rabble a tall, athletic guy with olive skin and tanned complexion and meticulously groomed spiked hair who was still wearing his old high school sports jacket scooped Jessie up from the waist with minimal ease before proceeding to spin her around.

"Let go of me" Jessie furiously protested as she grabbed the man's forearms in an attempt to break free from the former jocks grip whilst his friends laughed and jeered him on, in their blinkered view of the world they revered him as if he was an idol.

"Put me down you jerk" Jessie called again as the remaining customers sat watching the tense situation unfolding before them none wanting to intervene, finally he listened to her protests and placed her back on the ground whilst still yielding a smug and sanctimonious grin, as if Jessie really had wanted him to do it. "What the hell do you think you're doing here?" she spat pushing him away as he tried to pull her towards him.

"To see my girl" he returned trying to take hold of her again.

Perplexed with what he had said Jessie scoffed. "I'm not your girl, I haven't been your girl for nine months…now I'm telling you one last time leave me alone".

The restaurant fell silent as Jessie's ex boyfriend was stunned by her sheer nerve to reject him, one look toward his companions told them not to make eye contact, they chose the floor as a safer place to gaze upon, feeling emasculated the tall blunt object searched for someone to release his frustrations upon, instantly he picked Charlie who was trying to focus on the location of the noise as his vision had started to return in to focus.

"Hey, you" he called causing Charlie to look at him. "You got a problem buddy?" he waited for a response but it didn't come, Charlie just continued to stare. "What the hell are you looking at?".
"Leave him out of it Gill and get out" shrieked Jessie whilst trying to stop him from going anywhere near Charlie who was still struggling to formulate a reply.
"Noth…Nothing" he stammered finally finding his voice.
"That's right nothing…make sure you keep it that way" Gill threatened pointing his arm over Jessie's shoulder.
Feeling empowered Gill revelled in placing fear in others but that sensation was about to be short lived as suddenly he was grabbed by the collar of his jacket and dragged backwards, he turned as quick as was possible and was ready to explode and unleash hell on the perpetrator when he saw it was Caesar. In an instant Gill's temper was extinguished in to nothing his shoulders sank and his eyes became fixed on his shoes, even a blunt instrument such as Gill knew better than to infuriate Caesar who's squinted stare bore through him, he'd tested his patience once before and had immediately regretted doing so and Gill wasn't going to do it again.

"What do you think you're doing…coming in here and threatening my staff, my customers" his huge frame seemed bigger than ever, his massive arms folded and pressed against his large chest.
"We were just playing, that's all" Gill dared to look upwards to see an unimpressed Caesar who's stern and unnerving expression didn't show any signs of changing, it was as if it was carved in stone.
"We're just having a little fun" Gill was trying his best to play down the severity of the situation he and his friends had caused.
"Fun…Eh?" Caesar grunted as Gill willingly nodded. "I don't think so, so why don't you and your friends leave before I lose my patience" his arms tensed and his hands began to clench in to fists as Caesar was becoming angry.
"Yeah…yeah, we were leaving anyway" Gill returned quick and with relief, aiming a hopeless look toward Jessie in an attempt for her to relent her stance and feel sorry for him, but it didn't work as the only expression he received back from her was one of loathing and distain.
The four men hurriedly left but Gill's voice could still be heard from outside whilst he trash talked about Caesar and Charlie, indicating he could have taken them if he'd felt like doing so, an excuse his friends willingly accepted and agreed with,
"Are you ok?" Caesar asked the rather flustered looking Jessie who nodded with a sigh whilst pushing her fringe from her now clammy forehead, she had tired of Gill and his attempts to win her back but she knew this wouldn't be the last she heard from him.

"I'm ok" she reiterated as she turned toward Charlie's booth but Charlie had gone leaving only a few creased dollars on the table to pay for the coffee and the meal that had never reached him. Jessie turned on the spot before heading for the restaurants exit, pushing open the door she looked up and down the street but Charlie was nowhere to be seen, he'd simply vanished unseen by anyone inside the diner.

Clutching the piece of paper with the directions to the hotel Charlie staggered from Maine Street trying to follow the street signs his hands shook violently as if in constant spasm whilst he yielded a strong compulsion to vomit, people walked by throwing Charlie rather unimpressed looks and glares assuming his was intoxicated, his mobility and coordination could have been construed a that of a drunks, his shoulders brushed and scraped against the brickwork of the buildings he passed, it was the only way he could keep himself upright.

By almost sheer luck Charlie stumbled across his destination. "The Dragon Glass Hotel" it was a small two storey building, a renovated house that only boasted six bedrooms, the wooden structure was painted in a pale blue and had a light brown slate roof with a white picket fence around the outside of a bright flowered lawn.
Stumbling up the four wooden steps and through the door Charlie struggled to the reception desk, stood behind it was a petite and healthily tanned red head who beamed a warm yet business like smile his way, her jade green jacket held a gold plated badge with the name Blair engraved upon it. "Good afternoon sir, you must be Charlie" her smile held fast upon her heavy made up complexion whilst her tone of voice was upbeat and professional.
Not waiting for Charlie to reply she continued. "Jessie rang ahead with your reservation, I have put you in room three, which is just up the stairs there and to the right" Blair gestured with her right hand whilst she clutched the key with a circular gold key ring in the other.
"Thanks" he struggled, his eyes transfixed on the key.
"That's no problem sir, now Jessie tells me that you're from London…I'd love to go, see the sights, the queen, Kate and William…do you know any royalty?" Blair was a constant torrent of questions but Charlie wasn't in any sort of sound mind to converse or exchange pleasantries, with the way he was feeling he hadn't the patience to falsify interest.
"STOP" Charlie called bringing Blair to an abrupt and sudden silence. "Stop…please, I am incredibly tired and just want to go to my room".
"Oh…ok" she returned a little irked by what she saw as a rather arrogant rudeness on Charlie's behalf. "Here's your key. Room three, I hope you enjoy your stay" Blair continued nowhere near as

welcoming as she been before as she dropped the key on the desk, Charlie didn't care scooping the key up in his hand he nodded in appreciation before turning his attention to the steep staircase that now confronted him.

Turning the key in the lock Charlie stumbled inside the door slamming to a close behind him, the double bed stood in the middle of the snug square shaped room its linen a neutral cream and white that matched the wallpaper. The room yielded a sophisticated yet minimalist quality highlighted further by the lack of soft furnishings, with only a long, refurbished vanity table yielding a small fridge beneath it and a flat screened television above whilst a small round table with two chairs laid before the slatted French doors that led to the balcony.

Feeling as if he was about to pass out Charlie made it to the en-suite bathroom, emptying the contents of his satchel in to the dry and freshly polished sink he grabbed a yellow tube of pills, popping two or three in to his mouth and scooping a handful of water from the tap to wash them down. Charlie then staggered back in to the room, to him it was spinning in both a volatile and uncontrollable manner, unable to keep upright he fell face down on the bed his breaths feeling heavy and hollow before everything turned to black, Charlie had passed out.

## Chapter Six

With a distorted snort and a sharp intake of breath Charlie opened his eyes to find himself still face down on the soft yet sturdy duck feathered bed, feeling the furthest he had ever felt from a human being, as if waking with the strongest of all hangovers he carefully raised his head to see the bright new days sun shining through the French doors beside him. With his clothes contorted from the way he had slept Charlie pulled free his phone from his trouser pocket to see it was 9.30am, he'd been a sleep for almost eighteen hours.

His throat was sore and dry and in serious need of fluids, glancing at the mini fridge he eased himself down from the bed and crawled to the small silver box beneath the vanity table before taking out a complimentary bottle of water.

Unscrewing the plastic cap and his back pressed against the wooden frame of the bed Charlie drank the water down hungrily as if he'd been denied it for days, allowing a little to escape from the corners of his mouth and causing a stream of droplets to run down to his chin.

Once satisfied and feeling nourished he laid the bottle on his lap whilst Charlie hadn't the will nor energy to move, sitting crossed legged he stared in to space catching his own reflection in the black screen of the television, he looked gaunt and withdrawn whilst feeling fatigued and lethargic but also an underlining fear at what had happened to him. His illness had never made him that sick before and being so far away from home only added to his anxiety, bringing him to the realisation that the more the cancer ate away at him the worst his symptoms and subsequently side effects would become.

Still a little shaky and precarious on his feet Charlie shuffled towards the bathroom, his hand flush to the bed as he tried to regain his balance he pulled off his T-shirt that felt as if it had become too tight for him to wear, clinging to his skin it brought a stifling and uncomfortable quality. Throwing it on the bed Charlie noticed something, his black travel case that he'd left at the diner in his hurry to leave was stood upright beside the door with a small white envelope balanced upon its top. Perplexed with how it had gotten there he promptly tore open the envelope and read the one sentenced letter inside aloud to himself.

"You left this in my truck. Jessie. X". The kind gesture drew a slight smile but not as much as the thought of putting on fresh clothes did.

Having a shower and changing his clothes Charlie felt a little more refreshed and as close to his normal self as he could, taking the required medication with the remaining water left in the bottle

Charlie's thoughts turned to the reason of why he had travelled to America in the first place, to find Robert.

Retrieving his laptop from the case he began searching Lamont's local directory, scrolling down a few pages to get to the H section until he saw, the details for Robert Halliday, the sight of his name and address brought out a sigh of relief in Charlie as it confirmed he still resided in Lamont. Snatching at the Dragon Glass Hotel branded notepad and pen from the bedside table he quickly scribbled down the address and phone number on the yellow paper before tearing the page free of the pad.

Preening himself with hair products in the mirror Charlie wanted to make sure he looked presentable, his hair styled to perfection and his clothes pristine and crease free he armed his satchel with everything he needed. He took the letters, the folder and Isabelle's journal, everything he wanted to show Robert to prove who he was, the last thing he wanted was the man he thought to be his father to think that he was some sort of stalker or psychopath.

With a mixture of nerves and excitement Charlie left the room, his mind awash with hopeful possibilities, he had planned the day when he would meet Robert in his mind ever since deciding to find him and now the day had arrived. Reaching the final few steps on the staircase he saw Blair standing behind the reception desk immediately feeling guilty with the way he had spoken to her the day before.

"Morning" he awkwardly smiled as Blair raised her head slightly to make eye contact.

"Good morning sir, I trust you slept well?" she almost droned returning her gaze back to the guest book and something seemingly more interesting than conversing with Charlie, the pleasant and warm welcoming demeanour of yesterday was non-existent, she had taken to heart the abrasive attitude in which Charlie had spoken to her.

"Very well…thank you, listen I want to apologise for how I behaved yesterday" he began knowing he could have handled the situation with a little more diplomacy no matter how ill he felt, he sort to thaw the frosty atmosphere between them. "I was having a really, really bad day and I think I had jetlag…but that's no excuse for how I spoke to you and for that I am sorry…I was hoping we could start again?"

Closing the guestbook Blair stood up and looked at the hopeful Charlie. "Thank you for the apology and I would like for us to start again" she offered her hand and Charlie readily took it, he had a few failings in his personality but needlessly hurting someone's feelings wasn't one of them.

"There's someone waiting to see you" continued Blair taking back her hand and pointing over his shoulder.

It was Jessie, she was sat across from reception and dressed in a blue top, black jeans and matching jacket, engrossed in her reality star swamped magazine and with white earphones plugging her ears she didn't notice Charlie until he was only a few feet away from her. Clambering upright from the deep and high arm chair pulling free her earphones as she did so.

"Hi" she smiled whilst miming a wave, an action she instantly regretted in an attempt to seem cool, calm and collected but her body teemed with a nervous energy that made it almost impossible to do so.

"Hello" Charlie replied watching as Jessie realised she was still holding the magazine, immediately feeling embarrassed at him seeing her guilty pleasure, she discarded it behind the back of the chair. A little lost for words her body tingled as if receiving a shot of adrenaline. "You're case" she blurted out losing the little composure she had in his company. "You left your case…and I brought it back" Jessie was becoming ever more tongue tied with every word she spoke.

"Yes, thank you for returning it" Charlie smiled. "I'm glad you are here, I wanted to apologise for leaving so abruptly yesterday".

"No it's me who should be apologising" she interjected quickly. "I'm sorry you got dragged in to that hot mess, but hey ex's…what are you going to do?" Jessie awkwardly shrugged trying to play down the previous days confrontation with Gill, the encounter had left her still reeling in anger and embarrassment.

"Don't worry about it…it wasn't your fault" said Charlie in his usual reassuring manner.

"I'm glad you feel that way but I still feel bad" said Jessie her hands clasped tightly together.

"That's why I'm here, I want to make it up to you".

"That's really not necessary".

"I have the day off work and my car outside, I will take you wherever you want to go…I'll be your tour guide" she insisted. "See it as my way of apologising" she continued as Charlie tried to think of an excuse to decline. "Come on, you have to be spontaneous once in a while…right?" Jessie was trying her best to sell Charlie on the idea of spending the day with her.

"I would but there's something I really need to do today" he exclaimed looking to his bag.

"Oh ok, then I'll drive you" said Jessie optimistically showing Charlie that she wasn't going to take no for an answer.

Charlie knew there was no way Jessie was going to let him leave the hotel without her and the last thing he wanted to do was tell her why he was really in Lamont due to his naturally private nature and the sensitivity of the subject. "I guess I can do that thing tomorrow" he relented thinking he had waited a long time and that one more day without contacting Robert wouldn't hurt.

"Really…are you sure?" Jessie asked her smile ever widening.

"Yeah, what the hell" he gestured as Jessie had captured his attention with her infectious zest and exuberant enthusiasm giving her an aurora that both intrigued and captivated Charlie.

Jumping in to the truck Jessie knew exactly where to take Charlie, heading to Lamont's national park where the town's annual fair was taking place, it was a massive community event to both highlight and commemorate the town's broad history, its people and the community spirit they all seemed to exude.

Huge banners stretched from tree to tree highlighting it was Lamont's 73$^{rd}$ time of holding the event, a large stage had been erected for a local talent show and beauty pageant to take place. Beyond it stood a funfair complete with Ferris wheel, ghost train and small roller coaster, everything was grand and over the top as the town aimed to show its visitors its affluence and that no expense had been spared.

Navigating between people eating and children carrying helium filled balloons tethered by string along the narrow corridor between the busy stalls either side, selling all sorts of things from souvenirs, useless trinkets and home preserves as well as there being coconut shies and shooting galleries offering stuffed toys and goldfishes as prizes, Jessie wanted to show Charlie everything who had experienced summer fates and funfairs before but nothing on this size and scale.

Taking to a vacant bench overlooking the festivities that enabled them to enjoy the ridiculously embarrassing and truly terrible acts that the talent show had to offer with an ice cream in hand, but before too long Charlie could sense that Jessie was itching to ask something, trying a few times to begin but stopping herself unable to formulate the words in to a coherent sentence.

"What's wrong?" Charlie asked offering her a helping hand whilst licking his swift defrosting ice cream cone.

"No…it's nothing" she insisted. "It's just"

"Go on" he urged.

"I can't figure you out Charlie, you talk but you don't really say anything" Jessie forced the words out in one breath feeling that if she didn't her head was about to explode, her words had left Charlie with a squinted and perplexed expression.

"We've spent this time together over the last two days and I still don't know anything about you" Jessie continued feeling a sudden urge to elaborate on her previous statement.

"Ok" said Charlie slowly, realising Jessie was right he had been in her company ever since arriving in Bakersfield, a kind gesture from a stranger on the side road had led to him been sat on what most people would consider a date and yet to Charlie she was still a stranger. "What do you want to know?" he turned his body in Jessie's direction, giving her his full attention and trying as natural as he could whilst in his mind he wondered what she was about to ask.

"I don't know" she shrugged suddenly feeling a little bashful. "Something…anything, tell me about your friends, your family back in London, a crazed ex girlfriend that you've travelled half the way around the world to escape from, just something about Charlie" she gestured exuberantly.

Sensing a slight tepid frustration and an eagerness to know more about him Charlie fought back his natural instincts of defensiveness and quest for privacy that he had used as an aid for self-preservation for the most of his life and did something he hadn't done for a long time Charlie began to talk about himself. Telling Jessie about his background from being raised by his grandparents to Tommy and Lydia, of how his mother had died when he was a baby and of never knowing his father. Charlie couldn't have stopped himself even if he had wanted to feeling an almost cathartic experience as he revealed his inner self and laying himself almost completely bare for Jessie who was enthralled to say the least. But even though Charlie found it soothing and somewhat therapeutic he stopped himself from telling her about Robert and of his terminal illness, deeming those subjects off limits to bring up in the infancy of a blossoming friendship.

"And that's me, now you" he half smiled as he watched Jessie struggle to get comfortable on the steel bench, sitting cross legged and brushing her hair back behind her ears.

"Well I was born in Arvin, it's a small town a few miles outside of Lamont, like you I never knew my dad, my crack head mother could never remember who he was, by the age of seven I was a ward of the state because her drug habit had spiralled out of control and she couldn't take care of me anymore" Jessie almost spat with bile with the thought of her mother, her usual laid back and approachable demeanour was nowhere to be seen as she sat stern and rigid.

"I was in a children's home for over two years before I was found a foster parent, a lady named Paulette who lived here in Lamont, that's when my life changed for the better, instead of living in a rancid apartment with vermin and not knowing where my next meal was coming from I found myself in a peaceful and loving atmosphere, I stayed with her until I graduated high school and left for college, once I'd finished I came back to Lamont and picked up some work at the diner, I thought it would be easy way to make money before I went travelling…but here I am eight years later" Jessie stopped herself realising in that moment just how long her plans had been put on hiatus, wondering where the time had gone and how she could have lost the last eight years without really noticing that life was passing her by.

"Wow…that's pretty pathetic, I'm almost thirty years old and still a waitress" she sighed in a deflated and self deprecating manner whilst all Charlie could do was offer her a reassuring smile.

As dusk approached and the sun began to set both Charlie and Jessie had relaxed in to one another's company, the more they talked the more they realised just how much they had in common from the same tastes in books, films and music to their pessimistic yet intrigued outlook they had on life, the awkward pauses and silences that had once plagued their conversations were now virtually non-existent, they were comfortable in each other's company, it was as if they had known one another for years rather than just a few days.

The exuberant firework display erupted and cascaded overhead as the fair reached its climatic finale signalling its end, heading back to the truck he and Jessie were soon heading back to the hotel with the sun beginning its decent on the horizon ahead only extenuating the tranquil and relaxed relationship they had forged in such a short amount of time.

Whilst Jessie concentrated on the road Charlie noticed something poking out from the glove compartment just before his knees, without thinking he retrieved the A4 size black leathered notebook with a red binding down its spine, examining the cover littered with doodles and drawings in silver marker.

"What's this?" he asked innocently beginning to finger through the first pages, immediately answering his own question as he began to read the poem on the first page.

Horrified Jessie reached for the book with her free hand whilst keeping control of the vehicle.

"Don't look in there" she sighed whilst reaching for it again as Charlie playfully moved it out of reach whilst continuing to read. "Don't read them…they are not very good" Jessie insisted whilst writhing uncomfortably in her seat as if Charlie was probing in to her very soul, enabling him to see her personality laid bare, her thoughts, dreams and fear laid upon the pages that he now had possession of.

Finishing the second page Charlie noticed just how uncomfortable Jessie had become, she was quiet and her petite and slender frame tense whilst her line of sight was fixed upon the ever darkening road ahead, he closed the book and put it back in the glove compartment.

"You're wrong you know" Charlie spoke hoping to grab the now quiet and visibly peeved driver.

"You're writing is good…really good in fact" his words drew a slight bashful smile from Jessie who was both flatted and embarrassed in equal measure.

"You have a real talent Jessie, have you ever thought about having them published?" Charlie's instincts and keen eye for undiscovered talent was what had allowed him to progress so fast in his career at Doors and Handley and his instincts had rarely let him down before.

"You're joking?" Jessie scoffed, easing a little back in her seat.

"This is my job, if I didn't think that you had talent I wouldn't have said so" Charlie spoke with an enthused vigour a feeling he always got when seeing a new body of work, literature was his drug of choice.

"Thank you, you're sweet but no" Jessie replied seeing how serious Charlie was. "They are just my hobby, they don't mean anything" her shoulders twitched as she spoke as if her skin was itching in her awkwardness. "Writing for me is like therapy" Jessie decided to explain why she had taken up writing in the first place. "I started when I still lived with my mom, it was a sort of coping mechanism during the bad times...I do it because it lets me escape in to my own world with my own thoughts and ideas" she elaborated as they pulled in to the Dragon Glasses driveway.

"I respect that, but I still think you have a gift" Charlie reiterated his point with enthusiasm.

With the radio still on low a longing glance was shared and their bodies turned toward one another as the moment was set, but as they edged further towards each other something in the back of Charlie's mind stopped him and in doing so scuppered the moment.

"I had a really great day" he offered. "Thank you".

"I did too" she replied trying to hide her disappointment at what could have been such a tender moment.

"Right, well...goodnight" he stumbled, closing the passenger door he headed for the steps of the hotel when he stopped himself from going in. "Hey" he called returning to the truck before Jessie had the chance to leave.

About to speak Charlie felt a lump forming in his throat and the radiant smile awaiting him did nothing to help quell the sudden surge of nervousness he was feeling in his extremities. "What are you doing tomorrow?" he finally found the ability of speech once more.

"I have to work" she replied with a down hearted shrug of the shoulders. "Why?" she asked intrigued.

"I was wondering if you wanted to do something together, that's all" said Charlie a little defeated.

"Well, why don't you come to the diner, you've still not tried the Caesar special" Jessie smiled wanting nothing more than to see Charlie again, quickly she tried to fathom a way for them to see one another, deeming her suggestion was the perfect solution.

His heart still thumped fast as Charlie's smile reappeared. "Great" he swiftly replied, sounding rather eager. "That sounds great".

"Great it's a date...well not a date, but...but" Jessie lost the ability of speech becoming immediately flustered, her pale skin changing to a light shade of pink. "I'm gonna go...I'll see you tomorrow" she almost called as a smile of nervous excitement was shared between them, Charlie watched her drive in to the night, his body teeming with an excitable energy as for the first time in a long time he felt alive and not defined by his illness.

Intoxicated by the woman who had picked him up by the side of the road and not just taken by her looks and personality but everything that made her, her, everything about her drew him like a moth to a flame giving Charlie an almost addicted sensation that he'd never experienced before which he liked immensely and all Charlie knew was he had to see more of her.

## Chapter Seven

After days became weeks the thoughts of meeting Robert became a distant memory to Charlie as the once strangers whom had met by the side of the highway quickly developed a strong friendship, an intimate bond that they slowly began to rely upon where they both challenged and stimulated the other in ways neither had been before.

A spark of something more lingered between them like a solitary light on an otherwise blackened street and yet neither had the courage to act upon their natural urges. The thought and fear of destroying everything they had forged seemed too special to be risked on a whim whilst there was the possibility of reciprocated feelings of affection.

Although Charlie and Jessie were not willing to act upon their urges and desires for one another, they spent every minute possible together, wanting to know all there was about the other no matter how small and insignificant the information was. In the process of doing so Charlie learned that Jessie's talents seemingly knew no end, not only was she a talented writer but she also sang, having a regular spot a few times a month at a bar in town and Charlie had been invited to watch her perform, an opportunity he wasn't going to pass up.

Running late Charlie hot footed it in to town, he'd decided to rest on his bed after taking his strong medication which became a mistake he rued as he had fallen asleep. On waking he checked his watch to see it was quarter past ten and so Charlie hoped he hadn't missed Jessie's entire set, asking for directions he finally saw the flashing neon sign of the Peachy Bow.

The Peachy Bow was a small square structure with booths lining either side of the room and a handful of tables and chairs pushed up to the almost obsolete dance floor before the stage. The bar was bustling and alive with fifty or so inebriated customers and the room itself was almost in complete darkness, all except for the slow flickering lanterns that were housed on every table and one spotlight aimed at the stage.

As Charlie entered the bar everyone was on their feet and in the middle of giving a rousing applause, navigating his way toward the bar between the clustered groups of cheering and hollering people he saw her. She was dressed in a black dress with silver sequins that hung just below the knee whilst her hair cascaded over her shoulders and an acoustic guitar in hand Jessie took a modest and appreciative bow. "Thank you" she smiled as through the sweeping spotlight that impaired her vision she saw Charlie, the sight of him only sort in widening her already toothy grin and a feeling of elation that he was finally there.

"As this is my final song tonight I'd like to dedicate it to someone special, someone I haven't known long but who has opened my eyes to a whole new world" Jessie's eyes were locked on Charlie whilst she spoke, a look that was electric and segregated them from everyone else in the building, in that moment it was as if no-one else was in the room but them.

"This one is for him".

Gently plucking at the strings on her guitar the bar fell back to silence as Jessie began her final song of the evening, leaning against the bar Charlie was awestruck as he listened to her heavenly voice, receiving his brown bottled beer from a harassed and hurried bar tender he wondered to himself if there was anything that Jessie couldn't do. Truly captivated he couldn't help but smile to himself but the special moment would be short lived as he noticed four heavily inebriated men to his left playfully jostling with one another whilst being loud and menacing.

Upon closer inspection Charlie realised it was Gill and his moronic band of idiots, none of them considered that they were ruining everyone else's evening with their childish antics as they played around barging in to people and knocking over their drinks as they did so.

Shaking his head in disbelief at the lack of courtesy and sheer disregard for the other patrons, he tried to shut them out and even though feeling frustrated and annoyed that they were ruining Jessie's set Charlie focused his attentions on the beautiful and intoxicating women before him.

Drawing the song to a close the bar erupted even louder than before the applause was deafening and Charlie was louder than most, once taking in the adulation Jessie headed off stage and made her way through the still cheering crowd, immediately sinking in to herself and becoming a little shy and bashful with the intense attention, she began to blush, seeing Charlie she hurriedly made her way to him, ignoring Gill as she passed although he tried to attract her attention.

"Hey" he called trying to reach out and grab her arm but being heavily drunk he missed by quite a margin almost falling over with the momentum and barely managed to stagger back upright.

"So what did you think?" Jessie beamed reaching Charlie, in her mind it was only his opinion that mattered to her.

"Beautiful, just beautiful" Charlie replied as the once shared longing look intensified in an instant, seeing it as the perfect moment Charlie cradled Jessie's face with one hand who allowed herself to be willingly drawn in, their lips were almost touching when suddenly Jessie felt herself been pulled away making the once precious moment lost.

"What the hell?" slurred Gill his hand fixed tightly around her slim forearm.

"Get off me" she shrieked whilst trying to pull free.

"We need to talk" Gill continued not taking heed of her protests.

"There's nothing to talk about" Jessie snarled back finally managing to break free as Gill almost toppled over. "There will never be anything to talk about, you're pathetic and you're wasted…just go home and sleep it off before you make an even bigger ass of yourself".

The sudden outburst and subsequent argument had drawn the entire bar in to a massing crowd as the tension seemed to peak, making the atmosphere become close and heavy as everybody eagerly anticipated what was going to happen next through a series of hushed whispers.

Obviously not listening Gill wouldn't leave Jessie alone in his alcohol addled thoughts he believed he would be able to change her mind. "I'm not leaving, you're my girl" he reiterated as Jessie shook her head, she was out of ideas for getting Gill to realise that she would never go back to him. Charlie had watched and listened as Jessie had tried to handle the situation, failing miserably in the process to get through to Gill and he'd finally had enough, this time he wasn't going to shy away from the inevitable confrontation.

"Leave her alone, she's not interested" he interjected standing between Jessie and Gill.

His interruption had worked and now Gill's attention was drawn upon him. "Stay out of this man, this don't concern you…I'm talking to my girl"

"I am not you're girl!" Jessie almost screeched in frustration from behind Charlie, knowing nothing she had said had even resonated in his head.

"And judging by the state of you…she's a lucky girl" smirked Charlie, his words reeking with sarcasm as he took a sip of his beer, trying to be as primitive and imposing as his counterpart was.

"Keep your nose out of our business…you don't know what you're talking about…you don't know me" Gill pointed toward Charlie trying to be threatening whilst still swaying as if he was on board a ship in bad weather.

"No I don't, but judging by your nineties boy band inspired spiked hair, the shirt your wearing is two sizes too small in an attempt to overemphasise your muscular physique and the high school football jacket you're still wearing is from what…ten years ago, when I'm guessing you were the quarterback and the most popular guy in school and now your nothing…barely hanging on to a reputation you once had whilst everyone else has moved on minus you and your craterous friends who haven't the guts to do so, so to answer your question, no I don't know you…and from what I've seen I really don't want to, now if you don't mind we are trying to have a drink in peace" vented Charlie as he and Jessie turned away from the staggered looking Gill and returned to the bar, his tirade had left the bar aghast and in silence except for the odd whisper and few mocking sniggers.

Charlie had left himself spent but exhilarated bringing him an adrenaline soaked feeling of euphoria that made him feel as if he could do anything he chose, even Jessie had been stunned in to silence from what she had just witnessed but was impressed and flattered that Charlie had come to her defence with such gallantry. Grasping his hand and squeezing it a few times she smiled rather coy, bashfully resting her head on his shoulder as the lights overhead flickered on to illuminate the bar. Gill was led towards the exit by his friends each a little embarrassed by the scathing attack in front of so many witnesses none more so than Gill. His pride had taken a serious dent which left him feeling humiliated, glancing back to see Jessie so close to the person who had caused it left Gill consumed with an untenable fury and as the red mist descended over him, he broke free of his friends he pushed passed several people in his way. Reaching the bar he sort retribution, pulling Charlie backwards from the stool he was sat on Gill threw a right fist that caught Charlie in the face, he hadn't seen it coming nor did he anticipate the two following blows that struck his cheek and chin.

"No...stop....stop" shrieked Jessie standing in Gill's way in an attempt to stop his attack but she was easily brushed to one side by her Neanderthal ex who was intent on releasing all of his anger and frustration out on his target. Charlie's legs buckled and felt like jelly as he lunged at Gill sending both men crashing to the ground in a melee of swinging limbs, neither were prepared to yield as they jostled for supremacy but as quick as it had started the fight was stopped with both men being pulled up and dragged away from one another. Both were red faced, flustered and teeming with adrenaline but it was Charlie who had come off worse from the confrontation with a cut beneath his right eye and a split lip. Helped on to a stool beside the bar Charlie felt disorientated while his heart pounded fast and his skin tingled with the last remnants of adrenaline as it left his body, all after effects from the physical encounter. A short yet well built man appeared from behind the bar wearing a black polo shirt supporting the bars logo on the breast with a shined bald head and menacing demeanour he examined Charlie before heading to Gill who was still being restrained by two members of the security team.

"Get him outta here" he ordered gesturing with his thumbs jutting over his shoulder.

"Wha...what the hell man?" Gill protested struggling yet failing to break free of the vice like grip of the two bouncers.

"I've warned you before Gill, you do not come in to my bar and start fights with my customers, now get out and don't come back" spoke the southern Texan bar owner, his deep dulcet tone was rife with authority and purpose as he watched Gill and his friends being forcibly removed from the premises.

"You better watch you're back, man" Gill almost shrieked his threat aimed at Charlie. "This isn't over do you hear me...this isn't over" his bile infused voice echoed out on to the street before the doors were slammed shut behind him.

Getting an ice pack from behind the bar Jessie set about helping Charlie who was still feeling invigorated from his first fight since he was seven years old in the playground. "Honestly I'm fine" he insisted as the freezing ice pack impacted his cheek.

Jessie wasn't too sure, harbouring a mixture of concern, guilt and a little anger. "What the hell were you thinking?" she called with frustration whilst inspecting the rest of his facial injuries. "Do you know how stupid that was, you could have been seriously hurt" she continued revealing her concern and fear of what could have happened. "But I suppose I should thank you…for helping me" Jessie shrugged, leaning in and lightly kissing him on the cheek.

"Anytime" Charlie grinned, still feeling pretty proud of himself.

"How's he doing?" asked a deep and warm male voice as Charlie felt a heavy heated swelling beginning to develop around his eye and mouth quickly coupled with a sharp, pained sensation.

"I think he's going to be alright…thanks to you Robert" returned Jessie.

The name Robert instantly pricked Charlie's ears, raising his head to see a proud standing man looking back at him with a courteous yet genuine looking smile, his well tanned complexion extenuated his bright white teeth and grey curling hair. It was him the man Charlie was searching for, a little older than his picture on the blurb of his book, an image Charlie had burned in to his memory.

Charlie felt as if he was star struck looking up at Robert Halliday his eyes wide and his mouth slightly ajar, his search had swiftly developed in to somewhat of an obsession since discovering Roberts identity and now he was standing just a few feet away from him but Charlie found himself rooted to the spot and almost mute in his surprise of seeing him.

"Charlie" spoke Jessie seeing him transfixed on the five foot ten inch frame of Robert, observing like an artists masterpiece.

"Yes…yes, I'm fine" Charlie replied with gusto immediately feeling as if he had to prove just how unaffected he was from the fight, he pushed himself on to his feet but immediately regretted his decision to do so. His head began to spin and delivering with it a woozy feeling that both disorientated him and affected his balance, stumbling over Robert and Jessie just managed to stop him from falling.

"I think you need to be checked over at the hospital son" instructed Robert helping Charlie back on to the stool.

"No…no, I'm fine honestly" he shrugged but his words weren't very convincing.

"Not another word" Robert demanded rather stout and with authority. "We can take my truck" he indicated to Jessie as standing at either side of Charlie they helped him to his feet once more.

Before he knew it he was being loaded in to the back of an old sky blue coloured Jeep and on his way to hospital, feeling dazed and his pain now paramount Charlie kept the ice pack pressed flush against his cheek.

"How you doing back there son?" asked Robert looking through his rear view mirror.

"I'm, ok" Charlie mumbled, the muscles in his jaw and cheek throbbed and had a pulsating quality. Hearing the word "Son" coming from Roberts's mouth felt odd, he was using it as an affectionate term to a male younger than himself, however Robert didn't know just how accurate he was in his choice of words.

"You're accent…English?" Robert asked receiving a slow nod from Charlie. "From the south?"

"London" Charlie answered hoping the mention of his home city would strike a cord with Robert.

"London" he exclaimed unknowingly taking the bait. "I thought so…you know I lectured there for a summer back in the 80's" he continued.

"Really…?" interrupted Jessie rather surprised. "I didn't know that"

"Oh…it was a long time ago" he answered. "So what part of the city are you from?" Robert returned his attention to Charlie.

But Charlie didn't reply as he was a mess physically because of the fight but also mentally, he couldn't bring himself to speak suddenly feeling awkward and embarrassed by his appearance, he hadn't planned for the first meeting with the man he thought to be his father to be at a bar brawl. Instead he remained quiet and listened to Robert and Jessie conversing, hoping to glean as much information from Robert as he could, absorbing everything he had to offer from his demeanour and characteristics to a little of his own personality.

Turning in to the entrance of a huge multi-storey hospital that teemed with light not only from the building but from the circular solar lights nested in the long and expertly kept flowerbeds, Jesse leapt from the Jeep and opened Charlie's door for him before proceeding to help him out unsure if he would be able to walk unaided, clutching his arm she led him toward the automatic sliding doors.

"I'll be fine from here" said Charlie stopping Jessie from proceeding any further.

"I'll come in with you" she encouraged, ignoring Charlie's wishes she tried to walk on.

"Would you stop" Charlie shouted losing his temper, knowing there was every chance that once faced with the doctors he would have to declare his illness and Charlie wasn't ready for Jessie to know that about him yet. "I can look after myself, I'm not a child Jessie"

"I don't think you're a child…I was just trying to help" she replied unsettled by Charlie's outburst, letting go of his arm.

"I know but I'll be fine" Charlie reassured seeing the hurt expression that she now yielded. "I'll call you tomorrow" he continued before kissing her on the cheek, reeling a little from the pain in his mouth as he did so.

"Ok, but make sure that you do" she instructed as a slight smile in reaction to Charlie's kiss became visible she headed back to the Jeep, giving Charlie one last look as she did so.

## Chapter Eight

Discharging himself in the early hours Charlie left the hospital feeling battered and bruised and with three medical strips beneath his eye, once back at the hotel he tentatively climbed in to bed but couldn't sleep whilst his body twitched and ached.
Not knowing whether it was yet another side effect of his illness, the hangover or from the fight with Gill, Charlie felt incredibly tender and sore, tossing and turning as his mind spun with thoughts of his first encounter with Robert. He was mad and frustrated with himself and his self confessed bumbling and inability to speak whilst only being three feet away from him as they drove to the hospital. Laying on his side he tried to make himself more comfortable watching the alarm clock on the bedside table as its green lights flickered whilst changing digits Charlie came to a decision he had to stop being a coward and bite the bullet, he had to talk to Robert.

Showered, dressed and with a new enthused vigour Charlie was ready to go, checking the time on his phone to see it was a little after ten he made sure he had his evidence, letters and the journal in his bag before heading out of the room. Allowing an elderly cleaning lady wearing a pink tabard and white curled hair to pass him with her trolley she gave him a rather shocked look, her gaze was fixed on the medical strips beneath his eye and his swollen lip that had begun to scab whilst deep black and purple bruising had shaded around the cuts.
Once outside and knowing a little more of Lamont's geography thanks to Jessie, Charlie was able to direct himself via street names, signposts and his own premade notes through the town leading him to the right neighbourhood. Walking down the designated street Charlie couldn't help admiring the three storey town houses that lined either side of the road, made of wooden structures with stone foundations and surrounded with oak trees and manicured shrubbery, in Charlie's mind they looked vintage and idyllic as if he had walked on to a movie set.
Checking the yellow paper twice whilst standing beside a white painted mail box Charlie was sure he'd reached his destination, he was a mixture of nerves, excitement, trepidation and fear whilst his legs felt heavy as if reluctant in their use. "Come on Charlie" he spoke aloud to himself. "Its time to man up, this is what everything has been building up to…stop being a maybe man and do it"
The pep talk had worked as he began to edge along the cobbled garden path noticing its boarders of colourful flowers on either side of two small well-kept and extremely lush gardens, standing on the porch his fingers were poised on the doorbell, Charlie was finally ready to tell Robert just who he was.

Finally he pressed the bell hearing the chime ringing from inside as he did so, Charlie looked around him, at the peaceful and child friendly neighbourhood whilst a sudden burst of nervous energy built steadily in his stomach. Suddenly he noticed a familiar looking vehicle parked behind the blue Jeep, the door opened for Charlie to see Jessie standing before him, with a look of shock that they both mirrored.

Removing the toast from her mouth Jessie spoke. "How are you?" she smiled examining his face with a grimace of sympathised pain of her own.

"I'm fine…it looks worse than it is" he replied, rather confused he looked over his shoulder toward the number on the mail box thinking that he'd made a navigational error.

"How did you know that I'd be here?" Jessie asked with a hopeful grin, thinking of the hardship Charlie must have gone through in his search for her.

"I…didn't" he replied once more trying not to sound too harsh. "I came to see Rob…" Charlie stopped in mid sentence as Robert appeared in the doorway, he'd come to investigate who was at the door.

"Well if it isn't the Lamont slugger" he grinned. "How are you son?" he asked his voice warm and with a rich tone of masculinity but also a fatherly compassion.

"I'm good…yeah never better" he answered trying to stand as proud as his slim frame would allow when a horrible thought entered his mind, looking between Robert and Jessie, Charlie was thinking the worst. "Are you related?" he quietly asked unsure if he really wanted to hear the answer.

"Oh…no" Jessie returned swiftly shaking her head.

"Jessie was fostered by my partner Paulette" Robert explained. "But she still comes every Sunday for breakfast…and to raid our refrigerator" he winked.

"Shut up" she laughed playfully shoving Robert as it became clear to Charlie that the two of them were really close and comfortable in each others company.

"Hey" sounded a high feminine voice from within the house. "You're breakfasts are getting cold"

"Would you like to join us?" asked Robert gesturing inside, realising they had been stood on the white wooded porch for some time.

"I wouldn't want to impose" Charlie replied wanting more than anything to join them inside but his instinctive politeness had taken over.

"You wouldn't be" Robert insisted. "Please come in".

Charlie readily accepted and was taken inside the house, guided through the narrow hallway he noticed a dozen or so framed photographs hooked to the floral wallpaper, they were of Robert and a slender bronzed woman with shoulder length hair and piercing blue eyes, the pictures seemed to chart their history from holidays, professional portraits and from family gatherings.

"Charlie" beamed Jessie excitedly as she ushered him in to the kitchen, bringing him face to face with the woman from the photographs. "This is Paulette" she continued proudly.

"Nice to meet you" he offered his hand to Paulette who had her hair tied back and was wearing a white vest top with long denim shorts.

"Nice to finally meet you Charlie, I've heard a lot about you" Paulette lightly shook the visibly nervous looking man's hand whilst sharing a slight smile with Jessie who had already filled her in on the handsome stranger from England.

Each sitting around the small kitchen table Charlie sipped his coffee whilst watching from the periphery of the tight unit before him, listening to them converse, joke and laugh about things he had no opinion or knowledge about only answering when spoken to, Charlie suddenly became overwhelmed feeling like a rabbit caught in the head lights and with his nerves getting the better of him he excused himself and headed for the second floor bathroom.

Splashing a handful of cold water on his face Charlie stared at his own disappointed reflection in the mirror above the basin, his dull and sunken expression made him frustrated and intolerable by his own instinctive cowardice that was all but consuming him once again.

Taking a few deep breaths to steady himself Charlie decided the moment was now, knowing if he delayed any further he would never do it, fighting the desire to run from the house and never look back, he hurried down the dark varnished wooden stairs hearing the voices from the kitchen getting louder and clearer the closer he got.

"Charlie, is everything alright?" Jessie asked once seeing him in the doorway looking on with a little concern in her tone, noticing he wasn't himself.

Charlie swiftly nodded in return to her question, his body felt as if it was tingling and shaking whilst a voice in his head seemed to bellow with authority. "Come on do it, get a grip and just do it".

Formulating the words Charlie finally managed to force them out. "Robert can I talk to you…in private?" his voice slightly quivered as he did so, three pairs of eyes now looked upon him with a sense of intrigue and confusion.

"Eh…sure" Robert replied glancing at both Paulette and Jessie whilst thinking Charlie's request seemed rather ominous, he rose from his chair and headed towards Charlie. "Let's go in to the living room".

With the door pulled to a close behind them Robert offered him a seat. "So, what's on your mind?" he asked with a tinge of innocence in his voice.

Charlie sat in silence for a few moments clutching his bag on his lap, the time had finally arrived to show his hand and reveal why he was really there. "I haven't been totally honest with you about why I'm in America" he began, looking to Robert who was reclining in his high backed red leather chair, his arms flexed upwards from the armrests providing support for his chin to rest upon.

"Go on" said Robert a little suspicious by the man he had just met and how he was acting.

Charlie readied himself to continue, his mouth dry. "Ok…well when you lectured in London thirty years ago you taught my mother…Isabelle Marshall".

Roberts naturally laid back demeanour rapidly changed immediately becoming frosty and aversive as the name he hadn't heard in decades brought with it memories once suppressed sporadically re-emerging in his mind's eye. Ushering himself forwards to the edge of his seat Robert was imprisoned within his own silence, his piercing eyes locked on Charlie whilst his index finger drummed against his lips.

"Its ok, I know you did…I've read her journal, I know you had a relationship with her" the more Charlie spoke the more he seemed to grow in confidence.

"Enough ok…enough" said Robert assertively, jetting upwards to his feet before beginning to pace back and forth, with immediate effect he'd taken a defensive stance. "That was thirty years ago…a mistake I've put behind me" he gasped trying not to raise his voice so as not to alert Paulette and Jessie, he continued to pace in front of Charlie his arms folded tight to his chest, feeling hot and flustered and guilty as if trying to hide something.

"A mistake?" called Charlie stunned by Roberts riposte, he almost leapt from his seat to confront him. "My mother was in love with you…and you call it a mistake?" Charlie's voice became louder and rife with a volatile emotion whist still processing the callousness that he was experiencing.

"Oh yeah, she loved me alright" Robert scoffed belligerently as the feelings he thought eradicated decades ago had returned with a vengeance.

"She was" Charlie protested. "She never got over loving you, even after you left her…she had your child for christ sake" he yelled uncontrollably, his words froze Robert to the spot as if casting him in stone, finally turning back to face Charlie who's body trembled and moisture began to form in to tears, he was fighting them back as publically crying wasn't a trait he'd ever shown.

Robert couldn't bare to look at him any longer. "No…no" he stated shaking his head, he didn't want to believe him whilst realising why he had thought Charlie had looked familiar to him, it was because of his likeness to Isabelle.

"I'm telling you the truth Robert, I'm you're son" Charlie almost pleaded for him to see reason through his hastened denial.

"No" he bellowed. "You can't be" Robert called whilst reaching for his crystal decanter of scotch from the nearby drinks cabinet, filling a tumbler midway and drinking it down in one gulp before refilling it again, he had never felt as shocked as he did in that moment, his mind a blur and filled with heartache and nostalgia.

"Ok…lets say for arguments sake that Isabelle did have a child, then why didn't she have the decency to tell me…eh, why has it taken three decades for you to come forward?" snapped Robert finishing another scotch whilst still harbouring doubt over Charlie's credentials.

"Because until a few months ago I didn't know that you existed" he tried to explain. "I was never told who my father was".

Finishing his third double scotch a feeling of artificial clarity helped Robert to make his mind up. "No, I'm not buying it" he spoke adamantly. "Now I don't know what game you are trying to play but it isn't going to work…I want you out of my house".

"Game?" Charlie called in disbelief to what he was hearing, he was unable to comprehend how someone who seemed so caring and genuine could become so cold, hurtful and bitterly heartless in no time at all. "I'm not playing any games', I've travelled half way around the world to meet you".

"And what for eh…if its money you're here for then you're out of luck because I don't have any" Robert spat accusingly believing Charlie's aim was financial.

"I don't need or want your money" sighed Charlie defeated, from the scenarios of the best and worst possible outcomes for their meetings this was a thousand times worse than he could have ever imagined. He realised in that moment that he'd entered in to searching for Robert through rose tinted glasses he hadn't put much thought in to the consequences of doing so.

"Do you know what…forget it" he continued knowing that trying to persuade him differently was futile, he picked up his bag and headed for the door, his hand poised on the circular brass handle.

"This was a waste of time, I wish I hadn't bothered to find you" he twisted the handle and headed back in to the hallway almost walking in to Jessie and Paulette who had been eavesdropping on the explosive argument.

"Then why did you?" boomed Robert following after him, red faced and flustered with his posture tight and tense.

Charlie turned from the front door. "Because I wanted to see…see for myself the man my mother had fallen in love with all those years ago, the man she wrote about believing him to be kind, gentle, loving and someone who truly loved her" as he spoke Robert lowered his head unable to keep eye contact anymore with Charlie who seethed with hatred and fury, a contempt he had never harboured for another fellow human being until now. "I guess I was as blinkered and misguided as she was".

Incensed and saddened in equal measure Charlie opened the door, ready to leave when he remembered the letters. "Here" he called throwing the bound bundle of envelopes and the journal at Robert's feet. "The letters you sent, professing you're love, the one's that you didn't get a reply from…my mother never received them".

Robert remained motionless looking down at the scattered letters that surrounded him feeling terrible and racked with guilt from how he had behaved whilst Jessie and Paulette stood dumbfounded from the information and admissions they had heard, wanting to ask a dozen or more questions that they felt deserved to be answered but yet they felt compelled to remain quiet.

"She died…she died still loving you…you son of a bitch" Charlie snapped as he exhaled a shallow breath whilst shaking his head in disappointment.

Roberts head reared upwards from the shock of hearing that Isabelle had passed, he'd naturally assumed that she had moved on with her life with someone her own age and that she was happy without him, the thought of her dying hadn't even entered his mind. "Charlie wait" he stammered. But it was too late Charlie was incomprehensively furious and was already out of the door. "Screw you, you son of a bitch" he called over his shoulder. "Screw you" his voice trembled as he made a hastened exit from the property and was soon out of sight.

Robert stood at the door with his arm outstretched and flush against its frame bereaved of everything but sadness and sorrow, immediately he felt disgusted with himself, with how he had acted and how he'd treated Charlie. Paulette gathered the letters and journal from the floor before heading to comfort him, gripping Roberts arm and resting her head on his shoulder she didn't know what to say or do to make him feel better or to console him.

"I gotta go" called Jessie pulling on her short denim jacket and grabbing her keys.

"Where?" called Paulette watching as she eased herself passed them in the doorway.

"To find Charlie, he's upset and he's alone" she exclaimed reaching the porch, brushing her hair from her face, she had only one objective in her mind and that was to get to Charlie.

"Jessie wait" called Paulette once more, in doing so momentarily stopping Jessie from leaving. "Maybe you should just give him some space". Paulette had the advantage of age and wisdom on her side, she thought Charlie would want some time to himself to calm down but Jessie wasn't listening.

"You don't understand, Charlie doesn't have anyone else, he's out there and he's on his own…I have to find him" and with that Jessie headed for her truck, pulling out of the driveway, her search for Charlie began.

## Chapter Nine

Jessie drove throughout Lamont in her search for Charlie but to no avail, checking the hotels and numerous bars on Maine Street, even the diner but no-one had seen him, hours passed but she wouldn't be deterred as her concern began to turn to worry thinking to herself that she had checked everywhere until suddenly she saw him, sitting cross legged on the bridge leading out of town.

With one hand holding his phone to his ear and the other pressed firmly against the back of his aching head Charlie looked down at the slow flowing lake below him whilst seeking solace from Tommy back home in London, he'd explained what had happened and how his plan had disastrously backfired and wanted some reassurance and comfort from the people who knew him the most.
"I'm not sure what I'm going to do" he replied to the question proposed by Tommy, looking over his shoulder he saw Jessie tentatively approaching. "I'll call you later Tom, give my love to Lydia" he hurriedly ended his call not wanting Jessie to hear their conversation as she took a seat beside him, allowing her legs to dangle free over the edge.
The awkwardness they had tried so hard to dispel had now returned with a vengeance bringing with it a stifling silence, it was as if they had just met all over again.
"Well…I've had less eventful breakfasts" Jessie sighed hoping her dry sense of humour would aid her in defusing the tension and awkward silence.
"You think this is funny?" Charlie snapped still raw from the both draining and emotional altercation with Robert, his aggressive tone startled Jessie somewhat.
"No I wasn't" she began shaking her head and immediately regretting trying to make light of Charlie's plight.
"Well I'm glad my life amuses you" he interrupted feeling scorned and rejected, the one emotion Charlie couldn't deal with was rejection having felt like he had been all of his life, clambering to his feet he began to walk away clapping the dry dirt and damp splinters of wood from his hands as he did so.
"I'm sorry, I didn't mean to" Jessie called after him, disliking the sullen side of Charlie's personality, something she had never seen from him before, she stood up with her hands flush by her sides and her hands clenched in to fists as she tried to stem the emotional despair that now surged like electricity through her body making her feel lost and impotent.

"Charlie, will you stop walking away from me" she called once more, this time as she did so her voice sounded croaky and broken. "Just…stop".

Charlie finally listened to her pleas and protest and stopped allowing her to catch up, his eyes dull and tired looking as if they'd lost their spark and zest that had first attracted Jessie to him, grabbing him at the elbows Jessie made sure she was commanding Charlie's full attention.

"We can sort this out…ok" she nodded reassuringly whilst tears collected in the corners of her eyes. "Robert's just in shock that's all…we all are".

Charlie shook his head with a venomous defiance. "No, he's made his feelings crystal clear, Robert can go to hell for all I care" he fought with everything he had not to show how he was really feeling but behind his stout and hardened exterior and behind the façade, he felt lost and broken.

Large and heavy droplets of rain began to descend from the ever blackening sky overhead, mirroring Charlie's mood perfectly as it struck against them on the way toward the eager and dry ground.

"Just give him a little time, he'll come around I know he will" Jessie pleaded nodding suggestively but her words fell on deaf ears.

"He can have all of the time he wants because I'm leaving" Charlie spoke with a steely certainty causing Jessie's eyes to widen instinctively with a bereaved shock.

"What? When?" she gasped forcing the words from her mouth even though she didn't want to say them out loud.

Charlie shrugged seemingly unaffected from the hurt and almost horrified expression that was presented before him. "Tonight, if I can" he answered, pouting like a petulant child that had just been told no.

"So soon" she exclaimed watching as Charlie nodded in confirmation.

"There's no point in me staying here anymore, I've got my answer…there's nothing here for me" his lifeless looking eyes surveyed the lush, green landscape, looking at anything that would stop his eyes meeting Jessie's who harboured a look of utter devastation by his heartless statement.

"Nothing?" she asked, her voice almost at a whimper whilst holding it together with what little hope she had left.

Charlie gathered the courage he needed to look at her once more fighting every instinct that told him not to say it. "No…nothing".

Jessie let go of him and began to compose herself. In an instant feelings of humiliation and stupidity on her part invaded her consciousness and clouded her judgement, she became furious with herself for being so unguarded and honest with Charlie who she thought was different from anyone else that she'd ever met. She had allowed him to see the real her instead of the hardened and rather closed off persona that she had adopted for most people so as not to reveal her vulnerabilities, she saw it as a mistake on her part, a mistake she promised herself she wouldn't be making again as her tough exterior returned to the forefront and took a hold once more.

"Well if there's nothing keeping you here, then maybe you should go" she now sounded steely cool and detached as she spoke, she'd been hurt by people in the past but she had never thought that Charlie would be one of them, using her sleeve to wipe away what was left of her tears from her puffy, swollen eyes, smudging her mascara as she did so.

Not waiting for Charlie to reply she headed back towards her truck, she turned to face him one last time whilst walking backwards her hands clasped together, her devastation hidden and self preservation her main objective. "I guess I won't be seeing you again…" she shrugged. "So, it was nice to meet you, I guess".

Getting in her truck she tried not to look toward Charlie who was still rooted to the spot as if petrified in stone as the heavy shower had swiftly gathered momentum, she pushed the gear lever in to drive and pulled away. Making sure she was a safe distance away from Charlie's line of sight Jessie broke down, sobbing uncontrollably and bereaved by the callousness of Charlie's actions and unfeeling behaviour she felt physically sick coupled with an all consuming grief and heartbreak like she had never experienced before.

As night drew in so did a merciless storm, the blackened sky a cacophony of light and sound, the rain lashed down like a tsunami saturating anything it touched in an instant whilst the bone bitingly cold wind whipped and whirled in every direction with a high howling pitch.

Safe and warm Jessie had made it home whilst the storm was still in its infancy, curled up on her small patterned sofa with a blanket over her legs and waist, listening to music on her I-Pod as she almost frantically scribbled in her notebook, the pained sensation that plagued her like a disease also delivered to her an almost infectious inspiration to pen her soul churning heartache to the page. Shutting out the world and retreating in to one of her own, making it one of words and meaning Jessie devoured the escapism that writing brought her, knowing no-one could hear nor infiltrate the inner sanctum of her thoughts but no matter how hard she tried the thought of Charlie would not leave the forefront of her mind.

Her old house creaked and groaned in the seemingly relentless storm as she noticed a darkened silhouette pass by her window, pulling free the earphones Jessie stood up and slowly headed toward the door cautiously she began to unchain it when a damp, white envelope was slid under the frame and landing on the mat. Seeing her name handwritten across the front, the ink slightly smudged by the rain water Jessie placed it in the back pocket of her jeans before twisting free the two locks on the door with a little more haste than before, intrigued by the delivery.

"Hey" she called in to the dark bleakness that surrounded her noticing it was harbouring a dark sunken figure. "Wait…who's out there?" she called again as the dull wind seemed to intensify with every passing moment, both aggressive and relentless.

It was Charlie, he walked back towards the steps of her roofed porch soaked to the skin, his clothes stuck to his slim frame, his hair flat to his head and with the excess rainwater rolling freely from his nose and chin.

"Oh" said Jessie not expecting it to be him. "What do you want?" she asked with a sound of coldness in her voice, her arms crossed firmly across her chest as she immediately adopted a defensive and closed off stance, she was still raw with pain and hurt from their earlier encounter on the bridge.

"I…I wanted to apologise" he stammered, his body tense and shaking with the cold. "For the way I treated you, I shouldn't have taken how I was feeling out on you…it was wrong of me" he continued pushing his hand through his hair in an attempt to rid it of the excess rainwater.

"Yeah, it was" Jessie agreed still keeping her stance and looking rather unimpressed with Charlie's attempted apology. "And what's this?" she asked producing the envelope and holding it by her thumb and fourth finger.

"That is the truth" Charlie answered changing her expression slightly to one that resembled curiosity. "I've spent the last few hours walking and thinking about everything and about you" he began to explain whilst Jessie's glance repeatedly changed from Charlie to the envelope with an instinctive desire to rip it open and read its contents.

"I think you deserve to know the things about me that I daren't say to you out loud and once you have read it I hope you can understand why I've done the things I have" Charlie shrugged with a slight yet hopeful smile, seeing Jessie's aggressive and steely demeanour relent slightly.

"Thank you" she spoke still trying to be distant and unapproachable with Charlie even though he'd given her the key to his very soul within the water soiled envelope.

"So…what will you do now…are you still leaving, I mean?" she asked daring to believe that Charlie's reappearance may lead to a change of heart on his decision to leave.

"I have to, I can't stay here after everything that has happened…I just can't" Charlie tried to explain to the glum and once again dejected looking Jessie before him, the hostile and aggressive treatment he'd been subjected to by Robert had left it impossible for Charlie to even comprehend the thought of staying in Lamont.

"Will you go back to England?" she asked receiving the same stinging feeling of rejection that she felt at the bridge.

"No…I think I'm going to stay in America for a while, maybe do a little travelling…I've always wanted to visit New York, so I might start there" he answered whilst Jessie nodded trying not to show her aggrieved disappointment by Charlie's imminent departure from Lamont and her life.

"Well I suppose this is goodbye…again" she awkwardly shrugged feeling the tingling sensation the almost icy wind brought to her goose bumped skin.

Charlie gave her a reluctant smile as he didn't want to leave her but in his mind there was no other option. "I guess it is, but before I go I have to tell you Jessie that even with everything that has happened I'm still glad that I came here… because I met you"

Charlie's declaration rocked her a little, unable to respond she watched him climb the few steps of the porch, her body itching with an excitable energy, he took her hand in his own it was cold and damp from the elements that engulfed the town. "You are the most incredibly amazing, smart and beautiful women I have ever met and you deserve all of the love and happiness this world has to offer just like how you have given it to me" he lightly kissed her on the cheek as Jessie's body trembled and her heart pounded so hard she thought it was going to burst through her chest. No-one had ever given her such beautiful compliments before, the power of the words delivered with them a triumphant euphoria but also a grim heartache as she knew she probably wouldn't hear them again.

Finally feeling ready to speak Jessie was immediately interrupted. "Please…don't say anything because I think it would break my heart if you were to do so" Charlie spoke softly not quite knowing what would happen if he heard her intoxicating tone, deeming it far safer if she didn't utter a word.

Nodding with a saddened acceptance she took in the last images her eyes would have of him as Charlie prepared to leave but as he placed his hand on the wooden rail he received a sudden and almost paralyzing pain to the head, stinging and burning as if his skull was on fire. His body lurched forwards slightly as he fought to keep a grip on the water slicked handrail, his feet made contact with the drenched and soft earth as the pain intensified further. Charlie hadn't experienced anything like it before an excruciating pain sharp and stinging, with his senses dulled and body coordination severely lacking he staggered in to the wild weathered night clutching the side of his head as if it was about to explode.

Watching from her porch with her arms tightly folded once again in an attempt to stem the chilling wind from her skin upset and yet humbled with Charlie's parting words she remained yielding a strong and composed exterior. Suddenly she realised something was wrong watching as Charlie had almost come to a stand still, with a bubbling feeling of concern beginning to ride up inside her telling her she needed to act.

But she was too late as suddenly Charlie fell to his knees and then on to his side. "CHARLIE!" Jessie screamed with panic and horror as without second thought she ran to him, immediately realising he was unconscious she cradled his head in her arms. "Wake up…please, oh god Charlie wake up" Jessie pleaded her panic beginning to consume her, pressing her fingers to his neck she found a slight and weak pulse. Rifling through her drenched clothes as the torrential rain seemed to fall at its hardest and the storm waged ever on overhead she found her phone, her slick and saturated fingers managed to dial the three digit number Jessie required to summon help.

Charlie regained consciousness momentarily his body numb of all feeling and the searing pain in his head slightly easing whilst his limbs and muscles twitched in his paralysis, seeing two navy blue cap wearing paramedics towering over him. As the sky flashed white overhead he had been lifted on to a stretcher, slowly closing then reopening his eyes he noticed the image he saw had changed to one of the inside of an ambulance with the drenched and panic stricken Jessie by his side, her muffled voice in his ears tried to provide him with comfort through her own tears as finally everything returned to black.

## Chapter Ten

The second hand of the metallic framed clocked ticked ever on in the desolate waiting room as the storm outside eased in to nothing but drizzle, Jessie was sat alone traumatised and exhausted with her clothes uncomfortable from the still drying rain water and her hair damp and dishevelled. Waiting anxiously for news of Charlie who upon arrival at the accident and emergency department had been rushed in to theatre, looking to the monotonous ticking clock it was 3.32am, the three minutes since she had last checked had seemed like an hour.

Jessie's head throbbed as if a jack hammer raged inside her skull, the stress and fear of not knowing what was happening was almost too much to bare, the thought of Charlie laying on a theatre table whilst surgeons examined him internally brought a strong feeling of nausea from her stomach to her throat. Resting her head in her hands her heart raced as if ready to break free of her chest cavity, Jessie's breaths became shallow as she tried to calm herself but the traumatic events from the night before seemed locked in her memory and showing no sign of leaving her anytime soon.

Peeking between the gaps in her fingers she watched as her legs danced and twitched involuntary as if they had a mind of their own when suddenly the sound of voices emanated to her right and drew her attention. Turning sharply Jessie saw two nurses one in her early twenties, the other was at least three decades older, idly chatting beside the dimly lit nurses station whilst they checked through the awaiting patient charts.

Finding the strength to move her heavy lumbering limbs Jessie shuffled toward the nurse's station her body felt as if it had been drained of all energy making her reactions and responses dull and lethargic. "Excuse me" she quietly interrupted her arms folded against her cool and uncomfortable clothes as she spoke.

"Can I help?" asked the younger of the two nurses, trying to sound as helpful as she could, the heavy bags under her eyes revealed to Jessie she had been working a long shift, the once tight bun of blonde locks had begun to loosen on the young women's head whilst her once pristine appearance was now over half a day old the only thing keeping her going was a dangerously high level of caffeine in her system.

"I came in with a man about…six hours ago, he was rushed in to theatre and I haven't heard anything since" Jessie replied desperate for news of Charlie, no matter how little the information was, she just needed something, anything that would let her know he was going to be alright.

"His name?" the older nurse interrupted with a grumble taking to a squeaky desk chair in front of the computer, her spectacles peaked on the edge of her nose from the slight chain around her neck. "His name, my dear" she asked again, running low on both caffeine and patience.

"Charlie" Jessie swiftly replied, her elbows resting on the high polished counter as she nervously prepared herself for what was going to appear on the screen of the monitor.

"Charlie…what's his surname?" the nurse asked with a sigh, her thoughts already on her warm bed her tired bloodshot eyes peered over her pink framed glasses and straight at Jessie who awkwardly flicked her bottom lip with her finger.

"I…don't…know" she slowly replied once more as in that moment she realised that all of the time she and Charlie had spent together and the feelings that burnt with such a ferocity for him inside of her she didn't even know his last name.

"Umm" the unimpressed sounding nurse mumbled removing her glasses and allowing them to fall back on to her chest, the chain stopping them from going any further, she raised her eyebrows whilst armed with a tirade of questions ready to be released as she sought to find the patient, but as she was about to begin two singular bleeps from the flashing pager attached to her hip diverted her attention, she was needed elsewhere.

As she hurriedly disappeared on to another desolate corridor Jessie was escorted back to her seat by the nurse only a few years younger than herself but to Jessie she seemed older, not in appearance but in attitude and maturity.

Seeing how exhausted Jessie looked but also wrecked and ravished with emotional torment the nurse returned to her station and began to make several calls to each department in the hospital in an attempt to find where Charlie was, returning a few minutes later with a cup of reheated and terrible tasting coffee.

"Here" she offered with a smile, handing the cup to Jessie.

"Anything?" she asked hopefully, receiving a slight and cautious nod in return.

"I found your friend Mr Marshall…Charlie" she began her voice oozing compassion as Jessie eagerly listened. "He came out of surgery just under an hour ago, he's stable but still in a critical condition" she explained taking Jessie's hand in her own.

"But he's going to be alright…isn't he?" she gasped feeling her hand tighten around the nurses as she felt the surge of panic beginning to strike once more.

"I'm afraid I can't answer that" she answered sympathetically. "I've told the surgical team that you're here and the chief surgeon Mr Lawson is going to come and speak with you" she concluded as the phone at the nurses station began to ring.

"Thank you" Jessie mustered as the nurse headed to answer the still ringing phone, watching as she conversed for a few moments before hurrying away, something urgent required her immediate attention thought Jessie as she sipped at the strong, tepid sludge in the floral mug between her hands, grimacing at the taste and texture it left in her mouth.

Finding herself alone in the drab waiting room once more, bereaved of life and with only old magazines and the previous days newspapers for entertainment, how many thousands had sat where she was all hoping the for the same euphoric and panic eradicating news that a loved one was ok she wondered to herself. Jessie felt as if she was in purgatory knowing the emergency surgery was over and that Charlie was stable but nothing else, it was the uncertainty of what had happened to Charlie that required him to have surgery in the first place that seemed to reek havoc the most in her already chaotic ridden mind.

Time dragged slowly on as Jessie's exhaustion was getting the better of her, pulling her legs up on to the slim steel framed chair she covered herself with a blanket given by the paramedics in the ambulance, but no matter how hard she tried she was incredibly uncomfortable. Knowing it was all she had Jessie made do, her eyes felt sore and heavy as she rested her head on her forearm.

Falling asleep for no more than ten minutes she was promptly awoken by a firm yet gentle shake of the shoulder, sitting bolt upright her torso tense from the sudden awakening Jessie saw she had been joined by a middle aged doctor looming over her in green scrubs and white overcoat, his laminated I.D badge was clipped to his breast pocket along with three different coloured pens. He had a bronze California tan and a shock of grey running through his dark well groomed hair but still the doctor looked tired, a pitfall of working the night shift in the ER.

"I'm Mr Lawson, are you with Mr Marshall?" he spoke softly watching as Jessie stretched her limbs.

"Yeah…yes" she stammered realising when he referred to Mr Marshall the surgeon meant Charlie. "How is he?" she continued this time more assured and awake.

Mr Lawson took to the chair beside her his limbs welcomed the rest as he opened the folder in his hand revealing a dozen or so pages of information he had gleaned from the personal effects Charlie had in his wallet. His pink driving licence was held by a paper clip in the top left corner of the first page, the youthful picture of Charlie took Jessie aback slightly as he was almost unrecognisable with messy thick hair full of volume, healthy peach coloured skin and the bright and unyielding spark he had in his eyes, full of vigour that was almost non-existent in the Charlie she knew. The photograph made Jessie think what could have happened in the few short years since it was taken to cause such a change in Charlie's appearance.

"Mr Marshall has suffered a rather substantial brain bleed around the Parietal lobe at the front of the brain" Mr Lawson began to explain seeing the sight of all consuming terror in Jessie's eyes, a sight he had seen a thousand times in the eyes of his patients and loved ones but his stout professionalism allowed him to continue no matter what emotion was vented his way.

"The haemorrhage is a type of stroke caused by an artery bursting in the brain, allowing the localised blood to spread to the surrounding tissues and cells"

"Oh my god" Jessie shrieked, her body trembling with the words brain bleed, haemorrhage and stroke spiralled in her mind. "Please tell me he's going to be alright" the glimmer of hope that still resided within her was beginning to diminish once realising the severity of Charlie's injuries.

"It's too early to know anything for certain at this point" he replied. "Charlie has been placed under sedation whilst we continue to monitor his condition, we're using both corticosteroids and diuretics to counteract any reversible damage whilst we wait for the swelling around the brain to go down" Lawson explained further.

Jessie's stress levels had risen significantly while she listened to the diagnosis but now she had reached her breaking point, delivering with it an untenable panic that seemed to devour any rational sense or thought, she clasped both hands behind her head whilst she leaned forwards toward her knees, she had no idea how to process the information nor the feelings that came with it.

"Normally a cerebral bleed is rare" Mr Lawson continued hardened to a relatives reactions. "But they are more common with Mr Marshall's condition, this risk is more significant especially if he becomes overly stressed or is placed in a prolonged emotional state" he concluded.

Jessie's twitching appendages stopped as her head raised to make eye contact with the surgeon, something he'd said had resonated with her. "Condition?" she asked looking a little confused and perplexed with her eyes slightly narrowing to a squint. "What condition?"

Lawson's once helpful and compassionate expression drew from his face leaving one of slight bafflement. "You are Mr Marshall's partner aren't you…or his next of kin?" he quickly asked becoming increasingly uncomfortable, the folder quickly closed shut with his hand rested on top.

"Well no…not exactly" she shrugged with her reply whilst rubbing her hands together awkwardly.

"Then I'm sorry but I shouldn't be discussing this with you" Lawson returned with the medical code of conduct resounding in his head as he readied himself to leave, knowing the mistake he had made could be professionally damning.

"Please" Jessie almost yelped as she gripped his forearm, stopping Lawson from moving any further away.

"I'm sorry…but I can't" the surgeons voice dropped to a whisper as he tried to explain the awkward position he now found himself in.

"Please…I know I'm not his girlfriend or his family, but I'm the only person he has" she was almost to the stage of begging for Mr Lawson to recant on his confidential stance.

He sat for a moment in thought with his conscience dancing between relenting and keeping silent, looking at the both terrified and pained expression that the women yielded before him her frown lines deepened in her skin with every moment that passed, glancing out of the baron waiting room and passed the dimly lit nurses station, making sure that no-one was around as Mr Lawson decided to divulge.

"Mr Marshall has what is called a Metastatic tumour, it's a cancerous tumour to the frontal lobe of the brain" he explained as softly as he could the tragic reality that Charlie was suffering.

Jessie's jaw dropped and her mouth hung open, aghast by the mere mention of the "C" word, every fear and thought had now intensified a thousand fold as the deathly severity of Charlie's condition struck her like a wrecking ball.

"The tumour is removable though…I mean you can operate?" Jessie indicated to the surgeon with an insistent nod, the last of her hope now rested on Lawson's response.

"With the aggressiveness in the tumours growth and position, I'm afraid not" Lawson's words instantly condemned Jessie to a harrowing despair.

"How am I going to tell Charlie?" she gasped talking to herself out loud, her hands clasped to her face. "What am I going to say?".

"I think Mr Marshall already knows about his condition" hoping in a way his words would ease Jessie of her harrowing problem but only succeeded in bringing a distained stare from her in reply.

"When he was admitted my team found two packets of medication in his possession, both are prescribed to help with the pain and side effects of the illness" he explained to a still visibly shocked Jessie who was still having trouble believing Charlie was suffering from such a serious illness and he hadn't told her about it.

"I'm waiting for his medical records to be e-mailed to me from his physicians in England but I'm guessing he has been receiving treatment for this illness for some time" he concluded as the older nurse Jessie had encountered at the nurses station abruptly appeared with a strong odour of cigarette smoke clinging to her pink scrubs covered over with a sweet and cheap perfume in an attempt to hide her secret vice.

She handed Lawson his next patient's medical chart before sloping away back in to the corridor.

"I'm sorry" said Lawson hinting to her that he had to leave, standing upright whilst swiftly perusing his new notes, the plan for his next surgery already beginning to form in his almost mechanical functioning brain. "Will you be alright…is there someone we can call for you?" he asked his voice teemed with a natural compassion.

Jessie was only half listening as she was lost in her own thoughts, she felt lost like a child not quite knowing where to go or what to do next. "Eh…no, I'll be ok" she managed to reply as Lawson walked away. "Hey wait" she called easily catching up to him in the corridor. "Can I see him?". Lawson stopped and checked his gold and diamond faced Rolex to see it was nearing 4.30am, he knew no-one would be on duty for a few more hours to complain about contravening the visiting time policy. "Ok, but not for long" he instructed, watching Jessie nod in compliance before continuing. "This way" he gestured with a jerk of his head, indicating Jessie to follow.

Leading her through the corridors of the third floor they reached a ward of private rooms. "Room 6 and remember not long" Lawson reiterated almost at a whisper before turning around and heading back in the direction they had come.

Once inside Jessie closed the heavy brown door, with her back pressed firmly against the hard wood she peered in to the dimly lit room only illuminated by the beside light that shone like a halo over Charlie. Jessie stared at the tubes and wires protruding from his mouth and body and a white bandage wrapped around the top of his head whilst the only noise was provided by the bleeping flashing lights from the machines keeping observation over him.

Jessie felt as if she was falling apart crouching down she sobbed silently at the desperate and harrowing sight before her, a sight she could had never prepared herself for, her body shook uncontrollably as she felt like her heart had been torn from her chest, she had never seen anything like what was before her except for in the movies but with it really happening Jessie quickly realised she couldn't cope.

Eventually she made it to the bed resting herself on its edge beside Charlie, her body still slowly convulsed and her cheeks were sticky with still drying tears, Jessie was drained and exhausted both physically and mentally. As she watched over the unconscious Charlie time seemed to stop and being with him once more began to put her at ease, lightly taking his hand in her own she caressed his skin with her thumb.

"You are such a selfish ass, why didn't you tell me, you selfish…" she spoke out loud venting her frustration at him, in the hope the sound of her peeved voice would make him suddenly awaken. "Why couldn't you have told me?" she brought her face close to his hand before kissing it.

Resting back on the steel frame of the bed Jessie heard a crunch of paper instinctively reaching around she felt the sharp edge of folded paper in the back pocket of her jeans, pulling it free to examine it further she realised it was the letter Charlie had left for her, with what subsequently happened after its delivery she had totally forgotten about it.

Leaving the bed she took to a large green fabric chair beside the window using the moon that peeked in through the half open blinds as her light she tore open the re-dried envelope and retrieved the letter inside, taking a deep breath she unfolded the yellow papered Dragon Glassed labelled correspondence and began to read.

"*Jessie, this is probably the hardest letter I have ever had to write but here goes, when I came to America I hoped to find my father and try to form some sort of relationship with him and now I know that is no longer a possibility. But I want you to know that given the chance I would do it all over again because I got to meet you, the most amazing women I have ever met and I'm sorry for everything that happened between us, for the things I said and for the way I treated you I was wrong to do so and I hope that one day you'll be able to forgive me.*
*However I do have one regret with everything that has happened and that is that I can't spend any more time with you, in time wounds may heal but time is the one thing I have little of, because the truth is I'm ill. I was diagnosed a few months ago with a cancerous tumour on my brain, it's inoperable and has reduced my life to nothing more than a couple of months and it's because of this that I really have to leave. You have your whole life ahead of you to live and it breaks my heart that my passing will hurt you and so I've made the decision that in the long run my leaving will be easier for the both of us.*
*I will keep the memories of our time together with me until I draw my last breath and I want you to know Jessie that you were a light in the darkness for me and for that I am truly thankful. Forever in my thoughts. Charlie. X*

Refolding the paper Jessie's fingertips gripped the neat edges as her arched frame jutted up and down in the chair, struggling to draw breath she could no longer stifle her sobs. Her head reared up and Jessie caught sight of Charlie, holding her hand to her mouth it did nothing to help silence herself as she cried uncontrollably, she was no longer able to hold back the raw emotion she had sort to keep hidden and suppressed, all of her stress, trauma, panic and overwhelming fear exploded free from the shackles of her body.
Once able to stem the flow of tears and feeling as if she had used up all of the liquid her body had to offer Jessie managed to gather a little composure, allowing the release of her pent up frustration and feeling of helplessness had brought her an odd almost freeing sensation as if a weight had begun to lift from her chest.
Retaking her position by Charlie's bedside Jessie sat in silence just watching and hoping that at any moment Charlie would open his eyes and see her dotingly waiting by his side, but it wasn't to be as

a series of sudden raps sounded on the door indicating that her time with him was up. Leaning in Jessie left Charlie with a kiss to the crown of his head, it was the only place not bandaged before positioning her lips by his ear. "Come back to me Charlie" her whispers of instruction hadn't the effect she wished for.

She reluctantly headed for the door with the letter held in her grasp. "Please come back to me".

## Chapter Eleven

Hours turned in to days and the days passed to over a week with little change to Charlie's condition, Jessie had barely left his bedside only leaving the hospital to shower and change her clothes. She had made the small private room consisting of a bed, two cabinets and two high backed chairs a makeshift home, she slept in one of the chairs beside the window that overlooked a colourful memorial garden.

She spent her days talking to Charlie, telling him what was happening in the outside world, about the things they would do when he was able to leave hospital, she read aloud from the daily newspapers and every article from her gossip magazines as well as playing him music, Jessie was trying anything she could think of to try and evoke some sort of reaction, a spark that would rouse him back to consciousness.

By night Jessie spent her time watching Charlie sleep, nothing else mattered to her but being with him making everything except him and her fall in to insignificance. Without realising she had become incomprehensively devoted to making sure her face was the first Charlie saw when he eventually awoke.

With the warmth of the sun on bare skin, the sound of the droning mechanical bleeps of the machine and the intoxicating scent of fresh flowers in the nostrils, the fundamental senses sprang back in to action as Charlie's eye lashes twitched before his eyes finally opened, squinting at first as they adjusted to the bright morning sun. His nostrils became infused with sweet lavender as a nurse once seeing him awake leaned over to check the readings on the machine, Charlie tried to smile to indicate that he was alert and ok but the thick transparent tube that ran down his throat restricted him in doing so.

"It's alright" the nurse quietly cooed in an attempt to keep Charlie calm. "I'll go and fetch the doctor.

Charlie blinked slowly in reply his vision blurry as he found he was unable to move his head and neck both stiff, he'd been unconscious for eleven days and every limb and every muscle was tight and unyielding from lack of movement, although Charlie had been unconscious for well over a week he still felt incredibly drained and groggy as well as tender and tired.

The nurse quietly closed the door behind her leaving Charlie dazed and a little more than confused as he tried to piece together what had happened to place him in hospital, groaning a little as he writhed uncomfortably he heard a light sigh emanating to his left.

Navigating his gaze passed the table containing a few cards and two floating balloons each with the words "Get well soon" penned across their shining fronts he caught his first glimpse of Jessie since the night on her porch amid the frantic storm. His eyes widened in joy and surprise to see her curled up on a chair with a blanket tightly wrapped around her to the chin, she looked as sweet and as beautiful as she always did, the welcome surprise of Jessie being with him gave Charlie a warm feeling, a feeling that all would be well.

Suddenly a melody of light chimes and several vibrations emanated from Jessie's phone that sat beside her on the window ledge, sounding no more than a few seconds before she instinctively located and turned off her alarm with an outstretched hand, a few moments later she opened her eyes rubbing them with her hands before stretching her arms upwards and yawning.

She wasn't a morning person and it took a great deal of effort to motivate herself to move, pulling free the blanket to reveal her white and navy pyjamas when suddenly she saw Charlie staring back at her, it took a second or two for her brain to comprehend the sight she was seeing, hoping her eyes weren't playing tricks on her or that she wasn't dreaming after wanting this moment for so long.

Sitting upright her eyes wide and still not quite believing she slowly made her way toward the bed seeing Charlie straining himself to try and smile, staggered in awe and surprise Jessie brimmed with relief and elation to see him awake and back with the living.

"Nice of you to wake up" she retorted a dazzling bright smile revealed her all encompassing joy as she rested her elbows on the bed, getting as close to Charlie as she could without disturbing the tubes and electronic equipment that surrounded him.

With more effort than it usually took for him to raise his arm he delicately caressed her face and removed the solitary tear that slowly rolled to her cheek with his thumb, he was as happy as she was even though he was unable to show it.

Clutching his hand tightly her tears began to fall. "I thought I'd lost you" Jessie choked kissing his hand as a sudden rap of flesh on wood sounded on the door before the handle was turned.

Standing in the doorway was a tall and very well fed black man with a broad, welcoming and infectious smile and wearing a perfectly white lab coat. "Ah Mr Marshall, welcome back" his silvery grey moustache twitched as his smile widened. "I'm Dr Fenwick" he continued laying his medical chart at the base of the bed, his circular gold rimmed glasses poised perfectly on the wide bridge of his nose.

"You gave us quite a scare" said Fenwick as he checked Charlie's vital signs and reactions, deeming it safe to remove the pipe from his throat causing Charlie to wince and gag as the procedure was performed. Once it was clear of his airwave Charlie coughed a dry cough.

"Do you know where you are?" the doctor asked removing the latex gloves from his hands and placing them in the sanitised bin beside him.

Charlie nodded before trying to speak. "Hospital" he sounded croaky, his vocal chords felt rough and alien as if not his own.

Fenwick poured a small cup of water before helping Charlie to drink some, almost immediately the cool liquid brought relief to his sore and inflamed windpipe and thorax.

"Do you know why you're in hospital?" he continued taking away the cup once Charlie signalled that he'd had enough.

Charlie had an idea that his illness was to blame but he was still interested to know the specific reason behind what had happened to him. Dr Fenwick proceeded to tell him about the brain bleed and how they had kept him sedated for the swelling to decrease around the frontal lobe so they could see if there had been any damage excluding what the cancerous tumour had already caused. "You have been very lucky" stated Fenwick revising his notes on the medical chart. "Your last scan revealed that there doesn't seem to be any lasting damage to the Parietal lobe or to the surrounding tissue, it has begun to degrade but that is down to the Metastatic tumour" Fenwick concluded particularly upbeat on the prognosis.

By the mention of his illness Charlie's eyes widened almost panic stricken as he looked to Jessie who was still clutching his hand supportively, his stomach felt as if it was tightened in to a knot whilst the uncomfortable warmth of perspiration descended as he didn't know how Jessie was going to react by hearing the news of his terminal illness.

But she didn't react, her compassionate gaze unwavering. "Its alright I know" she finally spoke her voice teeming with its usual humility and warmth. "I read the letter" she explained feeling Charlie's fingers tighten a little more around her own, he felt a mixture of emotions relieved that Jessie finally knew his secret even though he hadn't had the guts to tell her himself but never the less happy there was now no secrets on his behalf between them.

Fenwick continued with his examination and his series of questions only bringing it to an end once feeling satisfied that Charlie was fully alert and in control of his faculties and responses, finally he detached the equipment that had been monitoring him whilst he slept giving Charlie a less restricted sensation.

The doctor left once his job was done his mind already focused on the next patient whilst a young male nursing assistant appeared, not saying a word or making eye contact he removed the machines from the private room, ready to redistribute them elsewhere in the hospital. Once alone Jessie carefully embraced Charlie being a little hesitant to apply much pressure on his still tender body, the feeling of warmth from his body was the only thing she desired after waiting for so long to hold him.

"I can't believe you're awake" she sighed at a whisper feeling Charlie's arm take a hold of her at the waist, holding her as close to him as he could. "I was terrified I'd never be able to talk to you again…never able to see you smile".

"I'm sorry that I scared you" Charlie croaked his voice still coarse and sore, the things he never wanted Jessie to feel was scared or hurt and that was the very thing he had caused her to feel.

"Its ok, you're back with me now and that's all that matters" she insisted trying to hide and avert the terrifying roller coaster of fear, dread and panic that she had been through but her eyes couldn't hide from Charlie just how affected and how traumatised she actually was by all that had happened. The harrowing, fatigued expression hidden behind her smile wretched at Charlie's heart and conscience, he felt responsible even though he'd been helpless to prevent it, still that didn't detract from the feeling of guilt that he administered himself.

With time, recuperation and Jessie by his side Charlie's health slowly began to improve, regaining his strength with each passing day, the rehabilitation he underwent coupled with the rebalancing of his medication soon had Charlie mobile again and well on the mend, the last remnants of his surgery had all but gone.

"Ah good morning Charlie…Jessie" the rich, warm voice of Dr Fenwick emanated from the slightly ajar door, his welcoming and naturally friendly demeanour was infectious. "I have some good news" he continued entering the room.

Charlie and Jessie were poised on the bed a little anxious with what the news could be. "What is it?" Jessie asked impatiently, looking from the doctor to Charlie and back again her body tensing slightly with anticipation whilst Charlie remained hopeful but quiet.

"Well… judging by how well the surgery went, how you're healing and how the medication has dealt with eradicating any swelling or residual blood I believe you can be discharged in the next day or two" concluded Fenwick enjoying the perk of the job he loved the most, telling his patients they were now well enough to go home, his enthusiasm and triumphant smile spread to Charlie and Jessie.

"Are you serious?" Charlie asked a little staggered with the thought of himself escaping the confines of the hospital, his words brought a sure nod from the doctor.

"That's fantastic" Jessie shrieked, leaping from the bed and hugging Fenwick, giving him a kiss on the cheek. "Thank you…for everything".

Charlie shook his hand. "Yes…thank you doctor"

"There's no thanks necessary" he replied believing his input in treating and rehabilitating Charlie was nothing more than any other doctor in his position would have done. "But I want to see you once a week" he ordered. "Because we don't want this to happen to you again" Dr Fenwick's voice changed to a tone of professionalism and authority.

"No problem" Charlie nodded readily, he would have agreed to anything if it meant he'd be free.

"And keep an eye on your medication, its imperative that you do so especially with your condition any fluctuation could be disastrous" Fenwick continued with his instructions.

"Oh he will, I'll make sure of it" Jessie interjected with a defiant nod, signalling to them both that she would be keeping a watchful eye over Charlie and his medication, making sure he would take them when required to do so. Feeling satisfied that his instructions would be followed Dr Fenwick left the soon to be vacant private room, receiving one last thank you from Charlie as he did so.

As morning became afternoon Charlie was in a buoyant mood with the prospect of leaving, the thought of feeling the sun on his skin and inhaling the crisp fresh air in his lungs only added to his anticipation. Taking down the well wishing cards from Blair at the hotel, Caesar and the unsigned third, he placed them in his bag along with several other belongings he knew he wouldn't be needing. But as he did so Charlie noticed something wasn't right with Jessie, she sat quietly on the bed intently watching her fingers as if they were about to do something amazing.

"What's wrong?" he asked carefully sitting beside her knowing Jessie's mind was definitely on something else.

"Its nothing…I'm fine" she returned hushed and reluctant to divulge what she wanted to say.

"Come on, what is it?" Charlie playfully continued to probe, still excited with the thought of leaving the hospital.

"I want to tell you something…but I don't want to make things weird or awkward between us" she finally answered looking a little awkward and insecure as she tried to decide whether to tell him or try and change the subject.

"Come on tell me…nothing you could say would make it weird between us, come on tell me" he smiled his voice rife with intrigue and insistence.

"I'm falling in love with you…ok" Jessie almost shouted as she blurted out her reply, the one thing she had wanted to tell him for days, Charlie's eyes widened and his smile faded, more so because of her delivery than the revelation. "I'm falling love with you" she repeated this time sounding softer and more feminine as her eyes finally met with his.

An all encompassing silence descended between them. "Well…say something" Jessie asked forcing an awkward smile but Charlie struggled to coagulate his speech, not quite knowing how to respond. "Please" she prompted for his riposte but it didn't come. "I knew telling you would make it weird, I knew it" biting her bottom lip Jessie wanted to kick herself feeling stupid for exposing how she felt only to be rejected by Charlie once again as she had been at the bridge.

"I'm gonna go" she announced, suddenly feeling claustrophobic as if she couldn't breathe with her embarrassment.

"Please don't go" Charlie finally spoke taking a hold of her hand in an attempt to stop her getting to her feet.

"Why not Charlie?" she sighed, her voice sounded tired, her eyes looked sad and dull as she awaited her reply.

"Because…" Charlie began steadying his nerve. "I'm in love with you too…and I have been from the first moment I met you on the highway" he explained as Jessie's mood altered almost in an instant. Her eyes regained their spark whilst the brightest of smiles jutted across her mouth, the feeling of elation felt as if it was erupting from every pour in her body, the words she had longed to hear from Charlie danced in her mind over and over again.

Jessie was happier than she had been in a long time, longer than she cared to remember but she couldn't help but notice the blank and unemotional expression that faced her. "Why do you look so sad?" she asked, for the life of her she couldn't understand how Charlie could be sad.

"I love you, more than I have ever loved anyone before and its breaking my heart knowing that nothing can come of it" he replied his head lowered in a defeatist manner.

"Nothing…" she gasped. "Why not?". Her joy was obliterated in an instant.

"Like I told you in the letter Jessie, it wouldn't be fair…on you, we both know I only have a couple of months…"

"Don't" interrupted Jessie the thought of losing Charlie left her with a burning sensation beneath the skin that felt as if it was going to tear her apart, but never the less Charlie knew he had to continue.

"I don't have long to live and the last thing I want is to know that I have left you hurt or broken hearted, no-one deserves that least of all you" he explained his reasoning as Jessie began to realise why Charlie had never really spoken of how he really felt, why he'd always seemed to stop himself at the last moment it was an attempt on his behalf to protect her from his inevitable end.

Sitting cross legged on the bed her body turned toward his, Jessie caressed Charlie's face with both hands as she drew him in closer until their noses were all but touching. "I know why you're doing this but what you don't seem to understand is that I would rather spend what little time we have loving you then spend the rest of my life without experiencing these feelings I have for you…I love you Charlie and I'm never going to leave you" Jessie's voice croaked and tears welled in her lower eyelids.

In that moment Charlie finally gave in to the yearnings he'd suppressed time and time again, this time Charlie wasn't going to stop himself from revealing what he really wanted taking a hold of Jessie he kissed her hard and passionately and Jessie welcomed his lips on hers like a desert welcomed the rain.

With their limbs entwined as they laid back on the bed the release of affection and emotion between them was intense and yet felt so natural, so organic and meant to be as if they had spent their lives waiting to find each other and now they had neither wanted to let the other go.

Spending hours in one another's arms their eyes longingly locked and the thought of protecting Jessie by leaving her a distant memory in Charlie's mind, nothing beyond the hospital room mattered it was as if they were cocooned from the world outside and both Jessie and Charlie was taking full advantage of their unique situation, for them it was as if time had stood still.

But their tranquil utopia was suddenly interrupted by the high pitched ringing of Jessie's phone, giggling as she reached for it whilst Charlie kissed her lips then cheek and then neck. "Stop it" she continued to giggle never wanting him to ever stop kissing her again because when he did Charlie made her feel desirable and special as if she was the only women in the world.

Sliding her finger across the screen to answer it. "Hello" she spoke looking to Charlie a little wide eyed as she listened to the voice on the other end of the line. "Err…no, I didn't forget" Jessie continued, by the look on her face Charlie could easily deduce that she had.

"Ok, ok I'll see you soon" she concluded allowing her phone to drop on to the bed.

"Damn I've got to go" she sighed rubbing her fingers through her hair, frustrated with her lapse of memory she usually prided herself on her organisation skills.

"Why?" Charlie asked a little startled whilst watching Jessie now rushing around the room, pulling on her jacket, boots and placing the strap of her bag over her shoulder before tying her hair in to a tight ponytail.

"That was Ron, from the bar" she explained pushing her slim cell phone in to her light blue jeans pocket. "I totally forgot but I'm supposed to be working tonight".

"Oh, ok" replied Charlie unable to mask his disappointment, not wanting her to leave.

Reluctantly Jessie knew she had to go leaning in she kissed Charlie, the novelty of doing so was something she never tired of doing. "I'll be back in a few hours" she insisted kissing Charlie again.

"I have something I want you to see" she continued retrieving her notebook from her bag and placing it on Charlie's lap.

"Your book?" he stated as three frown lines appeared upon his forehead whilst his eyes squinted slightly not quite understanding, he knew better than most just how protective and private she was over her writing.

"I wrote something while you were asleep" Jessie smiled heading for the door with a feeling of trepidation bubbling in the pit of her stomach as she gave Charlie permission to delve in to her very soul that she had poured on to the pages of the notebook he now had in his possession. "Let me know what you think when I get back" she called hurriedly as she left, knowing if she didn't hurry she was going to be late.

Positioning his pillows behind his shoulders and neck whilst pushing his glasses up to the bridge of his nose Charlie got himself comfortable in bed as he opened the notebook and began to read, his professional and insatiable appetite for literature instinctively kicked in as Charlie devoured every word, line and page until there was nothing left.

The lyrics Jessie had written were rather moving but her poetry was beautiful, filled with passion, angst, emotion and personality, Charlie knew how lucky he was to be able to see Jessie's most vulnerable side of her personality. She rarely revealed this to anyone but in her writing she left herself bare, smiling to himself Charlie felt vindicated in his previous opinion when he had read the first few pages in her truck that Jessie had an amazing talent and unutilised gift.

Rereading the poem Jesse had written especially for him Charlie was almost moved to tears by its fragility and delicate nature of fear and hope upon the precipice of the unknown, Charlie could see in a heartbeat the poem was about their own relationship.

A knock sounded on his door it was light, timid and a little hesitant to make too much noise but still engrossed in the book positioned on his lap Charlie wasn't paying much attention to anything else. "Come in" he called.

Hearing the handle turn and the door open Charlie continued to read assuming it was a nurse or assistant but when no voice sounded or any other noises resonated in his ears he looked up, in an instant the broad, heart-warmingly joyous smile that had been a fixture on his face since Jessie had told him that she loved him disintegrated in to nothing as before him was Robert and Paulette, standing awkwardly in the doorway with a bunch of flowers in hand.

"Hi" Robert dared himself to speak, his voice breaking slightly as he did so causing him to cough and clear his throat, his grip around the long stemmed bunch tightened as his body tensed in his anxiety.

Sensing Robert's panic Paulette loosely gripped his forearm whilst throwing him a reassuring glance that everything was ok whilst simulating the action for him to calm his breathing. "Hello Charlie" she smiled offering him a bright handled bag containing a gift perfectly wrapped with colourful wrapping tissue inside, seeing no gesture from Charlie to take it from her Paulette placed it at the foot of the bed.

"What do you want?" Charlie almost snarled with bitter bile, the warm and excitable mood had swiftly blackened, his eyes burnt with anger as if stoked embers in a fire.

The last person Charlie had ever thought he would see or want to see again was now stood before him with his common law wife for support, a vacuum of emotion whirled in his mind, all of them dark and embalmed in venom. Charlie had created such a hatred for Robert not just because of his rejection but for the cruel, insensitive and unjust manner in which he had done so, not just to Charlie but to the memory of his mother as well and now Robert was back in front of him and in Charlie's opinion looked withered and pathetic.

"I'm here to see you, son" Robert responded the panicked and somewhat pained expression unwavering on his face as he spoke, feeling clammy and uncomfortable and his mouth dry as if it had lost the ability to create saliva.

"Don't call me that" Charlie snapped like a bear trap, his finger pointing accusingly. "You have no right to call me that".

Charlie's arms were crossed and flush against his chest as he took a defensive stance, looking away toward the window with an expression of distain and disgust by the mere presence of Robert but yet a slight irking of curiosity resided no matter how hard Charlie tried to suppress it, a curiosity of why Robert made an appearance at all.

"How did you know I was here?" he begrudgingly asked making eye contact with Robert for only a moment before averting his gaze once more.

"Jessie" answered Paulette before Robert had the chance, the mention of Jessie's name caused him to turn sharply this time his eyes not moving from the blonde frame before him, a little startled and somewhat disbelieving.

"Jessie?" he repeated.

"Yes" Paulette nodded taking the advantage for her and Robert to edge themselves nearer to the chairs beside the bed. "She contacted us after your surgery and has kept us abreast of how you've been doing" she continued her hand resting on top of the coarse blue fabric of the visitors chairs. "I would have come to see you sooner but Jessie thought it better if I kept away, so as not to cause you anymore unnecessary distress but I've kept in constant contact with her, every hour of every day" Robert insisted finally re-finding his voice. "She showed me the letter" he continued, wincing with the thought of the letters contents, his pain readily heard in his voice.

Charlie's stare was as hardened as ever since their appearance at his doorway, he felt a little betrayed by Jessie's actions not only keeping them informed of his health but she had also told them about his terminal illness, without thought or consideration for his feelings on the subject. "What do you care?" Charlie spat his original stance of anger and disregard for Robert's presence never faltering. "Why don't you just get out…and leave me alone?".

Robert stood fast holding his nerve and taking to the seat beside the bed with Paulette by his side. "I'm so sorry Charlie, the way I acted was unforgiveable…but meeting with you shocked me by taking me back to a life I haven't lived in thirty years and I didn't know how to react" Robert tried to explain to the cold, stone like face of Charlie who looked over Roberts shoulder whilst nipping at his bottom lip with his teeth, seemingly emotionless and somewhat petulant, he didn't want to feel any sort of feeling or emotion for Roberts words.

Undeterred Robert continued he'd already prepared himself for a frosty reception before reaching the hospital. "I've read the letters and Isabelle's journal and I now understand what happened but you have to understand Charlie that for thirty years I had always believed Isabelle had rejected me…and that broke my heart".

Charlie pulled his knees close to his chest with his arms linking around them as finally his eyes met with Robert's, even though he didn't want to admit it he was intrigued and wanted to hear his explanation.

"After I had returned to America with no reply from Isabelle to my letters and what I thought was her rejecting me I fell apart, I started to drink thinking it would help me forget but it just made things worse, I lost everything, my marriage, my children and my job" Robert continued as Charlie's hard, ice cold exterior slowly began to thaw whilst hearing Roberts plight.

"My days grew darker and at their blackest I even tried to take my own life, a pill overdose got me admitted to a psychiatric hospital for treatment…and that is where my life began to change because that's where I met Paulette" he smiled to his partner who mirrored his expression whilst squeezing his hand, tears began forming in each of their eyes whilst Robert reminisced about how they met. "She was my support worker, she brought me back from the brink and helped me get clean" Robert beamed with pride at the women he thought to be his own private angel. "We became friends and ten years after we met we became a couple and for the first time in decades I was happy…I could see a future and a life I never thought possible again…then you arrived Charlie and without knowing brought with you all of the pain and memories of everything that had gone wrong in my life. Everything I had lost came back to me and I honestly didn't know how to process or cope with it so although I shouldn't have… I blamed you even though I knew it wasn't your fault" concluded Robert feeling a little drained and rushed as if he had but one chance to explain himself and didn't want to miss anything out. "I just hope that you can forgive me?"

For the first time Charlie began to see the situation from Robert's point of view, seeing the pain he had suffered from the perceived rejection of his mother and how it had almost destroyed him even taking him to the brink of suicide and making him think it was the only viable option to escape the despair that had ruined his life.

The sharp temper he'd inherited from his late grandmother had blinded Charlie from being able to think clearly after Robert's initial rejection, he hadn't stopped even for a second to think what sort of effect his appearance and revelation would have had on someone who didn't even know he existed, the perfect Hollywood movie ending had obscured Charlie's perception for any other outcome.

Watching as Robert's hands trembled nervously in Paulette's as he waited for his response to his detailed and soul bearing explanation Charlie felt like such an ass, annoyed at his own petulant behaviour, a trait that wasn't usually his own and one that irritated him in others. He had always been naturally stubborn but rudeness and being unnecessarily nasty wasn't, his actions delivered an immediate feeling of guilt and Charlie began to realise that he was being offered a second chance to start again with Robert to get to know his father with no secrets threatening to rear themselves from the shadows and with all of their cards on the table.

"So, what now?" Charlie asked his voice softened somewhat to its usual tone and pitch whilst his body language switched from closed off and defensive to a more open and welcoming position. "I just want a chance, a chance to get to know you Charlie, before it's too…" Robert stopped, finding himself unable to complete the sentence, feeling as if he wanted to wretch with its meaning as he sort reassurance and comfort from Paulette who was more than willing to provide it, Robert couldn't bring himself to address Charlie's illness in his mind never mind voicing it out-loud. "I just want to get to know my son…all I ask is for a chance to try" Robert finally felt comfortable to continue in his earnest plea, he stared at Charlie with a look of hope and optimism as his words had been delivered with a vehement passion.

The once angry and grudge toting Charlie who had yielded such a bitter anger toward Robert only minutes before was now contemplating the words. "My son" the words he had envisaged in his dreams and thoughts when he started on his journey. But now being addressed by that title gave him an almost joyous and euphoric sensation, a warm welcoming feeling like a warm coat on a winter's day or an embrace by a loved one that you hadn't seen in months.

"Well I guess we could try" he returned with a rye smile drawing gently from his thin lips. "I'd like that".

"Me too" Robert sighed with a glad relief, sharing a hopeful smile with his partner and son, feeling he had the chance of redemption, a chance Robert wouldn't let go as easy as he had done the last time.

With the elephant in the room addressed and a mutual line drawn in the sand Charlie, Robert and Paulette were able to speak freely, Robert eagerly lapped up every story and piece of information Charlie was willing to divulge with an unquenchable appetite. It was good start and a definite and significant improvement from their first attempt, each able to piece together a little more about one another's lives as they conversed further and openly enabling them to soon see that they shared quite a few character traits especially their personalities and sense of humour.

Opening up to one another more and more the conversation shared between father and son could have gone on all night but was brought to a close by the ringing of a high pitched yet softened bell not too dissimilar to a school bell, signalling that visiting time in the hospital had come to an end.

"I'll see you soon…son" beamed Robert with an almost ecstatic vigour with how the reconciliation had gone, shaking Charlie's hand he deemed it too soon to try and give him a hug whilst Paulette gave Charlie's shoulder a slight squeeze she too yielding a bright smile mostly out of joy to see Robert happier than she'd ever seen him.

"Ok" Charlie returned enjoying being referred to as someone's son, he hadn't experienced the term before but knew he would never tire of being called it.

"If you or Jessie need anything, just give us a call" instructed Paulette whilst Robert helped her on with her coat.

"Yes, anything" Robert interjected trying to sound as helpful as he could, with no task too big or small for him to undertake for his son.

"Thank you…really" smiled Charlie when suddenly he had an idea, "Well…there is something" he continued capturing their attention as they stood at the door, grabbing Jessie's notebook that laid beside him and offering it to Robert. "Can you photocopy me something?".

## Chapter Twelve

Once instructed vehemently by Dr Fenwick about the new strict timetable he would have to abide to with his new medication Charlie was finally discharged from the hospital thirteen days after being admitted. With his bag over his shoulder and Jessie holding his hand they headed outside, crossing the car park to the truck Charlie revelled in the bright sun overhead and the natural, healthy warmth it provided while his pasty and pale skin absorbed its rays for the vitamin D it lacked.

"Are you ok?" Jessie asked taking his bag from his shoulder tossing it in the back whilst Charlie seemingly glared in to space, a small grin drawn across his face.

Pulling Jessie in to his arms the grin was now a smile. "I have never been better…or happier and it's because of you" he confessed trailing her jaw line to her chin with his thumb, Jessie's porcelain skin felt like silk beneath his touch.

Leaning in to kiss her Charlie had never been as content, he had found a women he could have only dreamed of in the most unlikely of situations, Jessie had become his only constant in a painful existence and even knowing no long term future could be had she still wanted to be his all as he was hers, the one and only thing that mattered was the strongest emotion of all, love, unequivocal and un-apologising love.

As time swiftly passed on Charlie and Jessie settled with ease in to their new lives as a couple and though in its infancy to them it felt as if they had been together forever, moving in to Jessie's house they hadn't realised their acceleration to the relationship milestones. Subconsciously and with little thought they rushed to cram in as many aspects of a relationship spanning years in to the proceeding months, both wanting to live every new experience together before it was too late.

The same hastened approach had been applied between he and Robert, a day never passed without them seeing one another or at least speaking on the phone, learning through their lengthy conversations how eerily alike they were, whether through their mirrored humour or passion for literature even down to their stances on religion and countless other topics.

Intellectually they stimulated one another with mutual ideology and theories on a multitude of subjects and it was those key similarities that allowed them to develop a strong and unique relationship, a bond reserved only for a father and son. Charlie had finally found the thing he had spent his life without and for what most people took for granted Charlie had found a life, a life with a family and a women he loved, the very life he'd always dreamt of.

But as the chill of Autumn to Winter began its decent over California the second wind in health Charlie had experienced, credited in his mind to his new life and the people in it that brought with them the feeling of normality came to an end. The cancer was becoming too strong for his medication to counter act and suppress and before too long Charlie's health was in deterioration. A few days after celebrating his first thanksgiving the new string of grave symptoms began, at first removing his appetite and giving him a constant feeling of fatigue, making even the easiest of everyday tasks a struggle no matter how small, soon he became plagued by headaches that were constant and debilitating as well as spells of sporadic nausea and dizziness.

As time passed and with Charlie's health severely declining so much so that he could barely manage to get out of bed or use the bathroom unaided Jessie couldn't take anymore, she couldn't stand idly by watching the man she loved suffering in pained silence, she called for the doctor ignoring Charlie's protests that he would be alright and the doctor wasn't necessary.

Pacing the dark stained hardwood floor of her hallway Jessie waited for news beyond the sliding doors of the living room that had been converted in to their bedroom once Charlie could no longer climb the stairs, nervously she nibbled her thumbnail. Over the months since Charlie had been discharged from the hospital Jessie had taken it upon herself to almost become his nurse, monitoring and distributing his medications at the allocated times as instructed by Dr Fenwick whilst keeping an ever watchful eye over his health but for all of her newly researched knowledge on the disease gleaned from the internet Jessie was still unable to process and acknowledge the death sentence that hovered precariously over Charlie's head. Whenever the thought of him dying entered her head she managed to force it back out with her natural enthusiasm that had always given her hope, a hope that Charlie would be the exception, that he'd be the person to survive the terminal illness.

The door suddenly slid open and the round head of the general practitioner appeared, her blonde curled hair that resembled coiled springs sprang almost uncontrollably in her face. "You can come in now" said the G.P sounding solemn as she spoke, the latex gloves still on her hands from the examination.

Jessie tentatively entered seeing Charlie sitting upright in bed his bare back propped against the headboard, he managed a weakened smile as she sat beside him immediately clutching his hand, she was poised ready for Dr Surrane's prognosis.

"So give it to me doc" said Charlie his voice a little weary whilst still trying to be light hearted, he'd an idea of what the forth coming diagnosis was going to be.

Removing her glasses from her face Dr Surrane prepared herself to be the bearer of bad news. "All indications show that you are now in the latter stages of your illness…I'm sorry" the good doctor delivered the fatal and soul destroying news as emotionally detached as she could, she'd been treating Charlie for a few months and he'd easily become her favourite patient which made her job all the more difficult.

Jessie's head wretched towards Charlie with the feeling as if her world was about to fall apart, her entire body numb and rigid whilst her bottom lip quivered. "Are you sure?" she winced as she spoke receiving a slight nod of the head from Dr Surrane. "Surely there's something we can try…some experimental medication…just something" she pleaded still yielding hope for some sort of miracle cure to suddenly appear to make everything alright even though in her heart she knew there was nothing, her body trembled and she could no longer keep her composure.

"Hey, hey come here" ushered Charlie cocooning her with his arms as Jessie sobbed hysterically on his chest. "Its ok…everything will be ok" he lied in his reassurance kissing the crown of her head, Charlie was remarkably calm given the news but unknown to anyone he had long since readied himself for this day.

Once he had calmed Jessie enough to continue Charlie asked the question he dreaded to know the answer to. "How long…how long do I have?".

"A week…maybe two" Surrane quietly replied knowing the words were going to destroy the young couple.

Jessie's body still slowly convulsed whilst Charlie held her, she didn't want to hear anymore even with the time she had to prepare herself for the worst she still wasn't ready to hear it out loud.

"Oh…so soon" Charlie gulped unable to maintain eye contact anymore, staring at the bottom of the bed the unemotional and almost detached stance he'd hidden behind was now in tatters as his mind flooded with the thought of his own death, rendering him in a state of panic and fear.

"The pain?" he blurted out almost without thinking. "Before the end, will it be painful?".

"No" the GP reassured. "I'm going to prescribe you a stronger pain killer to help with that, and at the hospital…"

"I'm not going to the hospital" Charlie interrupted at a snap, his worse fear was to be confined to a hospital bed at the end of his life and he wasn't about to let that happen.

"Ok…alright" soothed Surrane. "We will install everything you need, right here at home, everything to make you comfortable" she ensured trying to eradicate the signs of blind panic and fear from Charlie's mind, the last thing she wanted was to add to the traumatising stress he was already going through.

"Thank you" Charlie mouthed silently whilst still cradling Jessie, he didn't want to upset her any further.

Dr Surrane quietly took her leave giving Charlie and Jessie the privacy they deserved, more than an hour passed without a word being exchanged between them laying in each others arms both trying to process and come to terms with what was now upon them, the impending end to everything they had forged.

"I don't know what to say?" whispered Jessie her head still rested on Charlie's chest, she felt drained emotionally aggrieved and heartbroken as she knew the little bubble she and Charlie had lived in for the past few months had burst and allowed the cold harshness of reality to creep in.

"It's ok" Charlie replied. "You don't have to say anything" he kissed her head the scent of her flowery shampoo lingered in his nostrils as he did so. Charlie didn't mind the quiet it allowed him to think to try and comprehend and to gather his thoughts.

"I had so many plans for us, so many things I wanted us to do and now we'll never have the chance" she whispered, around her eyes were dark black, her tears had caused her make up to run and now re-dried she resembled a panda. Climbing beneath the bed covers before reattaching herself to Charlie's torso, the chilling dusk weather had altered the temperature in the room.

"There's a cove on the beach of Santa Maria that I wanted to take you to, its isolated from the rest of the beach and so peaceful, the sea glistens with the sun's reflection and at dusk as the sun is about to set the ocean looks like shimmering silver" Jessie described with such a passion and yet her words were tainted with sadness, knowing that Charlie would never see the place that meant so much to her.

"It sounds beautiful" he smiled imagining the beauty of the solace cove in his mind from Jessie's description, he could almost feel the silver looking ocean at dusk lapping at his feet. "We'll have to go".

Jessie knew they never would but chose to believe and to invest in Charlie's words, grasping a hold of the idea that was now firmly on their to do list, a dream or not it gave them both something to hope for and look forward to.

Free of pain due to the increased strength of his medication Charlie felt a little more relaxed but his health was still deteriorating fast and over the following days he had become almost too weak to move and needing assistance with almost everything, the feeling of being incapable and useless frustrated him greatly and though untrue Charlie began to feel like he was becoming a burden.

A constant visual was kept by both Jessie and Robert at his bedside neither wanted to leave Charlie alone, absorbing everything they could glean from him before it was too late, Jessie had made a promise to herself not to cry or show just how heartbroken she was in front of Charlie only crying when she was alone, the last thing she wanted was for Charlie to see her falling apart from the strain of what was happening to him.

Knowing it could be their last chance to say goodbye Caesar and Blair came to see him both instantly devastated with how frail and painstakingly ill he had become in such a short space of time, it had been only a week since their last visits. But even more surprising to them was just how upbeat Charlie was, flippant and light hearted about the deathly disease that was devouring him with an unyielding appetite, he was trying to make them feel comfortable and at ease, wanting what could be their final words to be ones of happiness and jovial and not ones of sadness, he didn't want them to see the fear that constantly threatened to consume him.

But at night when he laid in bed with Jessie his fear was almost too much to bare his conscious thoughts changed sporadically between acceptance for what was to happen and an anger of how unfair it was for him to be dying so young, laid in the darkness with Jessie snuggled in close he contemplated mortality.

"Do you think there's something after death?" he asked aloud.

"Eh" moaned Jessie half asleep.

"Do you think there's something… up there, you know God, angels, heaven?" Charlie continued, he'd always been a stout atheist believing when your time is through on Earth that was it, but his rational fear had given him a change of heart, he hoped to be proved wrong, he hoped there would be something waiting for him after death.

Jessie clicked on the light beside her and rubbed her eyes she had been taken aback slightly by the sporadic nature and timing of the question but once seeing the eagerly hopeful expression greeting her opinion Jessie knew just how important her answer could be. "I think so, I mean I'd like to believe there is" she carefully crafted her response. "Why do you ask?" she continued a little confused she knew Charlie's stance and beliefs on religion and thought it was a little peculiar for him asking.

"It's nothing" he insisted with a smile. "I was just wondering that's all".

Switching off the light once more and snuggling back in for sleep Jessie realised why Charlie had really asked her the question, he was scared. "We spend such a short time living, there has to be something waiting for us when we go" she reassured, her view more certain and assured than her previous statement in an attempt to soothe and ease Charlie's worries. "What do you think?" she asked but her question didn't receive an answer. "Charlie" she spoke, this time a little louder but still nothing.

Thinking Charlie had fallen asleep Jessie closed her eyes placing her head back on to his chest but as she did so she realised something was wrong, Charlie's heart was racing and his skin had become cool and clammy, his body had tensed somewhat as if it was straining .

"Charlie?" she spoke again this time even louder than before, loud enough to have awoken him but yet again she still received no response.

Her hand frantically searched for the light switch a feeling of panic and dread searing through her body as she finally tripped the switch, unprepared for the sight before her, Charlie was having a seizure his body was convulsing, writhing and contorting uncontrollably.

"Charlie" Jessie shrieked, positioned on all fours as she yanked back the bed covers, straddling him she clasped her hands either side of his head. "Stay with me baby, stay with me" she wept her instructions, feeling redundant and helpless knowing what was happening to Charlie but powerless to stop it.

"ROBERT…PAULETTE" she screamed, her panic and terror made Jessie's voice sound even more pained and distraught than she already was.

Within moments Robert and Paulette burst through the door they had been sleeping upstairs, dishevelled and terrorised from hearing Jessie's screams they reached the bed they too knowing what was happening.

Pulling Jessie off the bed whilst she screeched hysterically Robert tried to check Charlie's vital signs opening his eyelids to see his pupils were almost fully dilated whilst his pulse was faint and weak.

"Come on son, come on" Roberts words were almost at a whisper as he silently prayed for his son to regain consciousness.

"Jessie, call the doctor" instructed Paulette who was trying to calm her. "Call Dr Surrane, tell her she needs to come here now…do it now" she almost bellowed to snap Jessie in to action, she ran from the room to make the emergency call.

The intensity of the seizure began to ease as Robert cradled his son in his arms, the convulsions slowed and became less aggressive. "Come on son…fight it come on, you can do it" Robert urged as tears silently fell from his face. "I can't lose you…not again" he continued stifling his desperation and frustration of not being able to do something to stop or stem the harrowing and painstaking situation. "It's not fair, none of this…we've just found each other and this disgusting disease is destroying everything that could be…and its just not fair" Robert spat with a bitter bile as he fell apart, breaking down in hysterical tears just as Jessie had done with the thought of his son's death rendering him to nothing, all of his strength and hope had been eradicated.

Dr Surrane burst through the door a mixture of day and sleep ware, no make up and her hair scrunched back and a dark medical bag in hand, quickly examining Charlie she was able to administer him something to slowly ease him out of the seizure, soon his rigid and contorted body relaxed back in to a more natural looking position.

Unconscious but becoming more relaxed Charlie's cold perspiration drew goose bumps to his skin as he lightly trembled, his breathing rather fast yet shallow as if his lungs were having to work overtime to provide the oxygen required.

"His heart rate and pulse are regulating" said Dr Surrane whilst rechecking his vitals. "But".

"But…But what?" Robert called his eyes were dark and sunken and becoming ever more agitated.

"I think you have to prepare yourselves" the doctor announced as she watched the small family unit that held one another for support crumble before her eyes. "Charlie has passed the point of return, I'm afraid he will only get worse as his health deteriorates" she continued to explain trying to remain professional even though all she wanted to do was cry herself.

"How…how long?" Jessie tried to ask sounding a little unemotional as she did so, she was working on auto pilot physically, mentally and emotionally destroyed and exhausted. "How long does Charlie have doctor?" she repeated trying to keep it together whilst all Robert and Paulette could do was watch, listen and hope.

"A day…two at the most" Dr Surrane answered once pushed for a response, watching as her statement caused them to recoil in sheer terror and heartbreak.

Robert's body shook as he cried out loud in Paulette's arms who was trying to comfort the broken man as he released all of his pent up despair, desolation and over bearing grief.

Jessie clutched Charlie's hand his pale knuckles resting on her lips, she was like a zombie bereaved of emotion, drained of everything that made her human. "Will he wake up…so I can say goodbye?" she asked her line of sight unwavering on Charlie, watching his chest inflate and deflate as he breathed.

"I can't be sure that Charlie will regain consciousness…with the severity of the seizure he suffered it could have caused too much damage to his brain…I'm sorry but he might never wake up" Dr Surrane's final revelation only aided their despair further, each not only had to face Charlie's imminent passing but also the prospect of not being able to say a proper goodbye.

With Dr Surrane making her leave, a bedside visual ensued each wanting to spend what little time they had left by Charlie's side, Jessie fell asleep beside him whilst Robert and Paulette occupied the chair, and in silence they held one another with a blanket over them to keep warm.

Shortly before dawn Jessie's eyes jetted open a feeling of frustration ripe in her mind, the last thing she had wanted was to have fallen asleep, and her eyes regained focus to see Charlie staring back at her with a smile, welcoming her back to the waking world.

"You're awake" she whispered gleefully, looking over her shoulder to see an empty chair, Robert and Paulette were nowhere to be seen. "How do you feel?" she continued instinctively leaning in to kiss him on the lips whilst brimming with elation and relief to see him awake his piercing blue eyes that made her feel warm and safe were tracked only on her, making Jessie feel like the only women in the world.

"I've felt better" Charlie groaned his head throbbing and his body numb, he felt as if he'd been hit by a truck, his body feeling like it was no longer his own, like he wasn't in control of it whilst the new and excruciating pain he was now subjected to was all encompassing.

"Why didn't you wake me?" she asked still a little annoyed with herself for falling asleep.

"I didn't want to wake you…you looked so peaceful" Charlie rasped his voice weak, he'd been awake a while but was content enough to watch Jessie sleep, taking the opportunity to take in her beauty whilst he still could.

"Good you're awake" sounded a voice behind them, it was Robert who was just managing to keep it together looking tired and dishevelled he handed Jessie a cup of coffee. "Everything's almost ready" he continued as Jessie noticed he'd gotten changed out of his pyjamas, his cheeks pinched pink from the brisk breeze of outside.

"Wait…" Jessie spat as she jostled with both speaking attempting to swallow the hot coffee. "What's almost ready?" she continued immediately suspicious as she looked to both Charlie and Robert in turn with a feeling of unease.

"We're going on a trip" Charlie answered trying to relieve the sudden expression of anxiety and confusion on her face.

"A trip, where?" Jessie tentatively asked, her exhausted brain lacking in rest and the ability of formulation.

"Santa Maria" Charlie explained with a rye smile, seeing his statement correlate in her mind. "I want to see the beach, the cove and the shimmering sea…before it's too late" he continued his staggered breathing caused him to stammer his words.

Rubbing his forearm before giving him another kiss Jessie understood. "Ok" she smiled kissing him again. "I'll go and get changed".

With Roberts Jeep loaded and ready to go they set off on the one hundred and twenty miles trip to Santa Maria, wrapped in a thick, woollen blanket Charlie's head rested against the frame of the open window, fighting to keep his weary eyes open he was determined to stay awake, taking in the passing landscape as the chilly almost bitterly cold breeze washed over him and blew through his hair, Charlie didn't mind the cold to him it evoked a feeling, a sensation that proved there was still a little life remaining within him and he sort to keep it for as long as he could.

Clutching his hand whilst their arms linked between one another's beneath the blanket Jessie's head rested on his shoulder, her mind was a blur of abundant emotion it felt unyielding, denying her even the slightest of capacity to comprehend even the easiest of questions or responses all she was able to think about was their journey would be Charlie's last.

The day was bright but still crisp and cool as they reached the secluded cove, hidden to anyone who didn't know of its existence on the Santa Maria shoreline it was a small piece of paradise, a private utopia unknown by the masses. Cocooned by the naturally misshapen rocks forged by millennia's long passed a small stretch of yellow and gold sand trailed to the ocean that beat unruly against the shore whilst foaming in the surf. Four chairs were erected and a small fire ignited within a self dug pit in the sand, the orange flames flickered and licked unyielding in all directions as if dancing in the breeze.

"You were right, it's beautiful here" smiled Charlie as his gaze devoured the natural beauty that surrounded him.

"I knew you'd love it" she forced a smile through the overwhelming despair that was consuming her.

Cradling a mug between her hands she watched the steam escape its porcelain rim whilst the curls of her hair tugged to be freed from beneath her woollen hat, she felt as fragile as a new born, delicate and vulnerable as she watched the man she love rapidly fading away before her eyes and she was powerless to prevent it.

With the blanket wrapped around him Charlie laid on the sand his head rested on Jessie's lap, his pale complexion had changed to a light shade of grey, still he fought against the incessant drowsiness that called to him like a lullaby. Hardly able to move or speak he watched and listened as his closest and dearest conversed, lapping up everything they had to say with an eager thirst whilst willing himself to make it to dusk.

The mood was heavy and sombre each knew time was short when suddenly Charlie began to cough as if he had something lodged in his throat causing his breaths to become short and shallow as painful tears trickled from his eyes, petrified Charlie could feel his body beginning to shut down like lights being turned off one switch at a time.

Rife and riddled with panic Robert and Paulette joined them on the sand knowing the time they had dreaded and willed not to arrive had come. "Don't fight it son…its ok" began Robert his voice trembled with his utter devastation. "Don't be scared…don't be scared" he tried to reassure though the thought of losing his son was tearing him apart.

"I'm not scared dad…I don't fear dying…because it has given me everything" Charlie managed to force the words out as breathing became even harder for him to do with every attempt. "If I hadn't been diagnosed with this illness then I wouldn't have met any of you…and in the time we've had together you have given me the life I've always wanted and I will always be thankful for that".

"I am so thankful that you found me Charlie, I am proud to be able to call you my boy…my son" sobbed Robert as he hovered over kissing him on the forehead. "You are my greatest achievement" he concluded hoping he had said everything he wanted Charlie to know and hear as he held on to Paulette like his life depended upon it.

Jessie remained quiet she didn't dare to speak, determined to keep it together for Charlie's sake even though she wanted the earth to swallow her whole and rid her of the pain and despair that resided like a volcano ready to erupt inside. Propping Charlie upright her chin rested on his shoulder with her arms under his and tight around his torso with a feeling of protectiveness she never wanted to let him to go as Paulette and an inconsolable Robert gave them a little time to themselves, moving further along the beach.

"I don't want to go" gasped Charlie revealing the overbearing fear that consumed him knowing he was no longer able to fight against the cancer that sort to take his life, his battle was almost over. "Jessie…I'm scared…I'm bloody terrified" Charlie confessed whilst wincing in agony, his senses had dulled and deserted his body leaving him with nothing but pain and fear.

"I know sweetheart, I'm scared too" Jessie finally replied still holding on to the man that she adored with everything she had, her body shook and trembled whilst she tried to conceal her grief and desperation.

"I want you to do something for me" spoke Charlie channelling what strength he had to speak.

"Anything" she whispered. "You know that".

"I need your word, that you will do what I ask…do you promise?" Charlie urged, grasping her hand in his.

"What for?" Jessie asked, perturbed by Charlie's ambiguous request.

"Do I have it?...please Jessie" his voice rasped as it strained making him sound panicked and irate.

"I promise" she finally mustered.

Once hearing what he needed Charlie began. "When I'm gone…" he stopped as if his words were choking him as they escaped but Charlie knew it had to be said and started again. "When I'm gone

I don't want you to mourn me, I don't want to die knowing that you will be heartbroken and unable to move on from this…I need you to keep living, to live a life that I can't".

His lungs were finding it almost impossible to produce oxygen only producing the slightest of morsels that kept Charlie going. "I want you to get married to someone who loves you as much as I do, I want you to travel the world, to have a dozen children and most important of all I want you to be happy…will you do that for me Jessie" Charlie concluded the air almost non-existent in his body whilst his head pounded as if trying to concave upon itself and spinning violently.

Jessie couldn't stifle the tsunami of emotion any longer her body convulsed uncontrollably as if a release valve had been turned on inside her, silently sobbing she formulated her response. "I promise…I promise"

Tears streamed down Jessie's face and her heart thudded so hard as if it was going to burst from her chest but the promise she had been urged to make had a seemingly calming effect on Charlie whose body had relaxed from its once frigid stance.

As dusk was upon them the grey shaded clouds overhead seemed to part and allowed the last remnants of the days sun to peak through and provide some much needed warmth as its delicate orange rays delivered the optical illusion of a shimmering silver texture in the choppy waters just as Jessie had described.

"I told you it was beautiful" she whispered kissing the side of Charlie's face. "Charlie…" Jessie spoke a little louder but still she didn't receive a reply.

Waiting a few moments Jessie silently prayed to hear Charlie's voice resonate in her ears but with it not coming she carefully moved her hand, it trembled as she lightly pressed her fingers against his neck, her greatest fear was confirmed, Charlie was gone

"No please no…Charlie" Jessie cried an almost inhuman shriek of soul destroying despair that had erupted from within. "Come back to me…please don't leave me" she wailed loudly, the hold around Charlie's limp and lifeless body only tightened in her reluctance to acknowledge that he had gone. Alerted by Jessie's screams of pain Robert and Paulette ran back to her, falling to their knees and without confirmation knew he had passed away, all racked in pain and grief their only consolation was that Charlie was finally at peace and free of the pain that had plagued him.

## Chapter Thirteen

A little less than a week after he passed Charlie was laid to rest with a small and intimate ceremony at St Augustine's church, an old yet beautiful building idyllic and with a nostalgia of a time long passed and yet its spiritual infrastructure seemed timeless.

The small procession of a dozen mourners followed the cobbled path through the compact graveyard of aged grey tombstones, their lettering faint and weathered as a cold nip resided in the air. Robert led the way inside his hand clasped in Paulette's as he trembled in his grief ridden pain a white handkerchief held to his mouth with his free hand.

Everyone filed inside all except Jessie who had stopped in front of the stoned arched doorway as if unable to cross the spiritual threshold her black dress made her feel constricted and uncomfortable as the thought of taking off her heels and running away circled in her mind.

"Come on…you're going to be ok" came a voice before her.

It was Lydia, Jessie had contacted her and Tommy to tell them of Charlie's fate, and even with her being seven months pregnant they made the long transatlantic journey to say their final goodbyes to their best friend. "We'll get through this together" she offered her a warm smile rife with a compassionate reassurance and a helping hand to guide her inside.

Leading Jessie who resembled a zombie, emotionally drained from the trauma she was still trying to comprehend to her seat beside Robert and Paulette, Lydia took to her own her black knee high dress emphasising her burgeoning baby bump. Resting her head on Tommy's shoulder she comforted her husband who was emotionally in tatters he'd rarely stopped crying since hearing the news Tommy's eyes were pink, swollen and bloodshot giving him a fragile and dispossessed expression.

The priest an old fair haired man well in to his sixties and dressed in full religious regalia commenced the regular formalities that were warranted for a funeral, a generic dialog he had repeated a hundred times before highlighting the importance of god and his master plan for all as well as speaking a little about Charlie from the information he'd gleaned from Jessie, Robert and Paulette.

"And now" the priests baritone voice resonated with a deep husk to the congregation. "Charlie's partner would like to say a few words" he continued looking to Jessie who seemed to be in a world of her own. A world where pain, sorrow and despair was the oxygen she breathed where there was no sun and no light just shadow and bleakness, a gentle squeeze of her forearm by Paulette brought her back to the living as she saw the old priest beckoning her forwards. Making it to her feet she slowly headed to the pulpit having to pass the dark wooded coffin that contained Charlie and with it everything she had ever wanted, her legs began to buckle as a light headed feeling made her feel faint, her small frame was sunken beneath her clothes making the jacket she wore seem to be too big like a child in an adults clothes.

Looking out at the saddened and tearful faces staring back none more so than Caesar whose huge solid stature was hunched forwards rising and falling at regular intervals whilst he sobbed uncontrollably, the mountainous man was inconsolable as he plunged a huge ball of tissues against his face in aid to stem the unrelenting flow of moisture.

Retrieving a folded piece of paper from her pocket Jessie readied herself to speak, it was the last thing she wanted to do as the solemn figure she cut was vulnerable and unprotected as a precariously unbalancing sensation rampaged through her veins.

"I only met Charlie eight months ago and yet it feels as though I have known him my whole life" she began her voice wavered as if she was about to burst in to tears. "Meeting him on the side of the road I knew instinctively that he was different from anyone I had ever met before and I was right. As I got to know him I realised just how special he was, Charlie didn't want pity or to be treated as if he was different, all he wanted was to be happy" she continued turning the page.

"He came to America knowing his time was short to find his dad and to find meaning of where he came from…to find who he was and in coming here I think he found more than he could have thought possible, because here in this little town Charlie found somewhere he belonged and a family of people who loved him…loved him for how special and loyal and amazing he truly was". Jessie had almost reached the bottom of the page knowing she had left the most heartfelt piece to the end.

"I had the fortune to have been loved by Charlie to be engulfed and enveloped by his unwavering and all encompassing love, a feeling I have never and may never experience again, the passion he had for everything he believed in was infectious, for love, for life and everything honest and beautiful…and I loved him, I loved him from the first moment I met him and I always will…I will miss him every day until I see him again".

Jessie finished, folding the paper in to a small square once more before replacing it in her pocket, she looked back out in to the church to see not a dry eye, each mourner had melted in to the pews clutching tissues and handkerchiefs to their faces as Jessie's speech had rendered each of them bereaved and inconsolable.

The musical intro of guitar strings being plucked sounded from the four small black speakers in each corner of the church as the scarlet red and gold embroidered curtain slowly began to close in front of the dark wooden box that contained Charlie as it readied to take him on his final journey.

With the ending of the song rendering the church in a heavy and glum silence slowly the small congregation made their way back outside, the once cold and bleak looking day had somewhat changed on their exit as the bright glow of the midday sun presided over a cloud free sky. Offering their condolences to Jessie, Robert and Paulette the mourners began to leave returning back to their ordinary lives a luxury they didn't have.

Standing with Lydia and Tommy, Jessie was suddenly embraced in a mass of muscle and warm flesh behind an ill fitting suit, the embrace was more like a grappling hold that you would find in a wrestling match as she was lifted up a little from the ground and the air forced from her lungs by Caesar.

"I'm so sorry…I loved London, he was a good man" sniffled Caesar still unable to contain himself.

"I know you did" Jessie comforted but couldn't help thinking that Caesar's tone was a little too high for a man of his size as he finally lowered her back to the ground.

"And I don't want you to worry about work…you can come back whenever you feel ready, there's no rush" Caesar continued rubbing his eyes with his engorged sausage like fingers.

"That's kind of you Caesar but I'm not coming back to the diner".

"What…why?" Caesar gasped a little shocked, his mouth slightly ajar from hearing her admission.

"I made a promise to Charlie that I was going to live…to experience everything this world has to offer and I'm not breaking that promise" she insisted with her explanation, the memory of being with Charlie on the beach for his final moments flashed in her minds eye whilst she spoke of him.

"I've been stuck in a rut for too long, lying dormant and becoming stagnant, waiting for something that would change my life, waiting for something new to come to me and I've realised that if I want something to happen, for my situation to change then I have to change it for myself" spoke Jessie with a resolute and determined passion.

"What will you do?" Caesar asked still rocked at the thought of losing her not as an employee but a friend.

"I don't know" she shrugged earnestly. "There's a whole world out there just waiting for me" she elaborated further with optimism.

"Oh…wow" Caesar forced a smile whilst sounding defeated. "But remember if you need anything, you know where to find me".

Caesar lurched away toward the white wooded gate at the exit of the graveyard as Jessie felt a slight spark of energy inside, a feeling she hadn't felt in a long time it was the feeling of excitement of the unknown and the same feeling of excitement she'd experienced when she had first met Charlie.

With arrangements already prepared to head back to Roberts and Paulette's house they headed towards their vehicles as a stranger approached, dressed in an expensive black tailored suit and reflective aviator sunglasses, his hair expertly cut and styled down to the last strand.

"Excuse me but are you Jessie Olivers?" he spoke revealing his British accent.

Intrigued but instantly suspicious Jessie closed the door to her truck. "Yeah" she finally answered exchanging glances with Tommy and Lydia. "Who wants to know?" she continued remembering seeing the man seated at the back of the church when she had delivered her farewell speech to Charlie.

"My name is Jason Kraft...I am a senior partner for the publishing house Doors and Handley of London, I was hoping I could have a moment of your time" he answered yielding a hopeful yet professional expression whilst handling Jessie his personal business card. "I used to work with Charlie, he was a good man and I give you my condolences for your loss".

"Thank you" accepted Jessie. "But how can I help you?" she asked still not quite understanding why he was there.

"Before Charlie passed he contacted me about you" Jason began, his words causing her eyes to narrow with confusion.

"He sent me a copy of your work...of your poetry, and I have to say you are incredibly talented" he elaborated further seeing the look of confusion swiftly change to one that resembled terror.

"My work...he gave you my work" Jessie reiterated instinctively becoming peeved with Charlie's actions and embarrassed that someone else had read her work without her knowledge, her private pursuit revealed to the world. "Wait, how could Charlie have sent you my poems, my book is always with me" Jessie asked a little argumentative and defensive, immediately assuming Jason had made a mistake.

"It was when Charlie was in the hospital" interrupted Paulette. "He gave Robert your notebook to copy...but he swore us to secrecy" she explained further to answer Jessie's questions whilst her mind mired and span as she tried to comprehend the information being thrown at her.

"Charlie always had a great eye for talent and both I and my employers completely agree with his opinion so that's why I'm here" Jason interjected bringing the conversation back to the matter at hand, placing his black leather briefcase on the bonnet of her truck before unlocking the two clasps and removing a thick A4 sized envelope.

"My employers want the opportunity to represent you and publish your work…in this envelope there is a contract offering you a three book deal".

Taking a hold of the envelope Jessie was in shock never in her wildest dreams could she have imagined what was being offered to her so readily, she stood aghast as if she had lost the ability of speech.

"It would be a great shame for your work to remain undiscovered but I also don't want to rush you in to a decision so please take a few days to think it over and give me a call" smiled Jason placing his sunglasses back over his eyes and shaking Jessie's hand.

Once Jason had left Jessie was hugged and embraced several times in celebration but she was in shock somewhat but something else staggered her further, that even after his death Charlie was still trying to help and push her further than she would have ever pushed herself.

Looking up to the azure blue sky overhead Jessie couldn't help but smile, she had chosen to believe that Charlie was watching over her, she wanted to make him proud and the drive he once had for a better life and for happiness was now her own and she was going to utilise the opportunity for the both of them.

## Epilogue
## One Year Later

The frost nipped in the air whilst the slow falling snow began to settle, floating to the ground upon a bustling London as Christmas was almost ready to make its annual appearance. Shoppers saddled with bags sort shelter beneath umbrellas whilst heading to their next retail destination, the roads were chaos as usual and the intent of settling snow only furthered the desires of the vehicles occupants to flee back to the suburbs of the sprawling metropolis. The air was polluted with the sounds of whining car horns and the argumentative voices of disgruntled drivers venting their frustrations at the red double tiered buses that seemed to engulf the roads and cause nothing but gridlock.

The snow had settled in the bottom corners of an old bookshops window proving a rather festive and peaceful view on the chaos taking a hold outside. A crowd of thirty had crammed themselves inside for the private reading, sitting enthralled and eager before a small lilac backed stage as Jessie read the finale of her new book, but it wasn't poetry it was the story that had changed her life.

"And that it was, Charlie died on the 2nd of December at 5.45 in the afternoon with everyone he held dear and loved beside him, his ashes were scattered through the ocean in Santa Maria, a place that he'd fallen in love with" read Jessie the projection of her voice both loud and warm as she enlightened her audience with what had happened after Charlie had died, taking a sip of water from her nearby glass she continued.

"Finally re-inspired, Robert began writing again, his latest novel has the academic world excited, he and Paulette are currently in Bavaria researching for his next book, Tommy and Lydia returned to London and six weeks almost to the day of Charlie's passing she gave birth to a baby girl whom they named Elizabeth Charlie, we still keep in touch but as for me I was given my dream, to become a writer and see the world, if it wasn't for Charlie that's what it would have stayed… a dream".

Closing the hardback book and resting her hand on the laminated jacket Jessie straightened the slight crease on the thigh of her navy trouser suit, her attire was professional yet feminine her dark curled hair cascaded freely over her shoulder as she looked out at the engrossed gathering who looked at her back each saddened yet happy their eyes swollen by tears already shed.

"That incredible and beautiful man who appeared from nowhere and changed my life had been handed a tough life from no fault of his own, though struck with a terminal illness he decided to embrace life, to take the bull by the horns and to find out who he was but in the process he'd changed so many lives for the better by simply being in his presence, not bleating or complaining about his health or the pain that the cancer brought. He found a small piece of this world that loved him unconditionally, he was a hero to some and an inspiration to others but to me he was the man I loved, the man I will continue to love until I draw my final breath and see him again, this is our story…the story of Charlie Marshall.

Printed in Poland
by Amazon Fulfillment
Poland Sp. z o.o., Wrocław